# STUDENT
# OF
# NO CONSEQUENCE

*This book is dedicated to all of my amazing grandchildren -
Kalei, Kya, Eliana, Olivia, Josiah and Tallulah.
They are the ones who will have to live their faith out in today's
changing culture.*

# STUDENT OF
# NO CONSEQUENCE

**DAN CHESNEY**

*Edited by Amber Grant*
*Published by Amazon Publishing*

# ACKNOWLEDGMENT

Published by Amazon Ebook

Scriptures taken from The Message Bible, 1993 by Eugene H.Peterson. Published in association with the literary agency of Alive Communications. P.O. Box 49068, Colorado Springs, CO. 80949

New King James Minister's Bible, Hendrickson Publishers, Inc. P.O.Box 3473, Peabody, MA 01961-3473, July 2006

New International Version, copyright 1996 by Zondervan Publishing House, Grand Rapids, Michigan 49530, U.S.A.

Good News Bible, The Bible Societies, Collins/Fontana, British usage edition first published 1976, Stonehill Green, Wrestle, Swindon SN5 7DG

An * over a word symbolises it is a slang word used in the fifties.

# TABLE OF CONTENTS

# CHAPTER 1

# HIS POLITICAL EGO

*"Why the big noise, nations? Why the mean plots, peoples?*
*Earth-leaders push for position, Demagogues and delegates meet*
*for summit talks…"*

*Psalm 2:1-2 MB*

"What are we doing up here?" Asked Jim.

Andy replied, "The same reason we're always in these global warming weather conditions, to protect some potential politician whose scheming on how to tax more of our money. And why are you so distracted tonight, your acting like an *odd ball?"

"I applied for an opening in the secret service, I guess I'm preoccupied with that. This agency has been limited in my view, it's been nothing but former foreign dignitaries, corporate big wigs and nobodies like tonight, haven't you wanted more? This feels Mickey Mouse* to me sometimes. Jim yelled out.

"I have, but I'm not letting it interfere with what we are here for right now. And by the way, I wouldn't have envisioned you being interested in prestige, or having your sights on the presidential duty?" Andy remarked as he looked over to see where Jim was. "Your rifle is getting wet, get back to your position and keep watch."

"Yea, Yea, keep your powder dry, there's assassins everywhere, and yes, you are on the right track, I don't want to spend my life babysitting potentials or washouts, I was meant for more than that. This is 1958 Jim, the whole world is exploding with opportunities and new discoveries. We now have computers, microchips, optic fibres and space rockets, and I want to be right in the middle of it all. That is if Khrushchev doesn't nuke us all." Than Jim sarcastically grunted as he moved back to his position. "You think

1

they'll assign us to his daughter, Catherine, I understand she's a *knockout with brains. ."

"No," said Andy, "a women will get that job. Besides, she's too young for you, and from what I've heard she's been graced with a social magnetism that rivals Grace Kelly."

Andy had seen Catherine's pictures and could tell this girl was going places, ambition and determination were written all over her face. It would take power, money and position to impress that girl. She was *unreal.

"By the way, what is globe warming?" Asked Jim.

Andy moved closer to Jim and said, "it's some new research the government is doing on CO2 emissions from cars and how its melting the poplar icecaps."

Jim remarked, "You mean the Eskimo's are going to be the new beachfront property owners, let's invest now and create a second Miami Beach, will be rolling in the *dough. But you know what's going to happen?"

"What?" Andy asked.

"Every time the government does a research project they always turn it into a new taxation and we will be the ones paying for refrigeration in the North Pole.

It was blindingly dark, the rain was unrelenting and from Jim's perspective this was a waste of specially trained personnel, but then again, this was the government. No other type of organization could waste more time, more resources and more *bread than government.

They were stationed on the roof of a Victorian five-story building opposite the new Danton Grover Hotel, designed in a chic contemporary art deco style, *modernism at it's best. It was the architectural jewel of the city. The all glass front made it easy for the two special branch men to guard and protect the politician's in the rooms opposite them.

Cars were approaching, everybody was alert, eyes concentrating, rifles pointed, sending of messages through their communication pieces and their fingers lightly touching the triggers on their Savage 110 BA sniper rifles.

First a Cadillac pulled up, then a limo, followed by a black Mercedes with government plates, as usual the special branch made a secret meeting all the more conspicuous by their choice of automobiles. Everyone exited from their vehicle and opened their umbrellas. The driver of the limo also jumped out and opened the back door where the Governor of Massachusetts slid out under a canopy of umbrellas. The rain made it more difficult to distinguish between who was who, everybody was wearing black raincoats with black hats under black umbrellas surrounded by black cars on a black night, making any kind of shot impossible, a small detail their superior didn't plan for. This caused Jim and Andy to start murmuring under their breath, their frustration boiling over with the occasional grunt. Within seconds they were all in the building making their way to the fifth floor. If it was anyone more important it could have been a black moment.

The Governor was use to attention and notoriety, but this level of recognition was beyond what he had enjoyed so far. He came to this clandestine meeting because when two senators from your party call from Washington and want to meet with you at midnight urgently, you know that your political career is either ending or being catapulted. And besides, who could resist finding out what they wanted. The conspiracy skeptic in him was too strong to pass up.

"Governor," said Senator Colin, "good of you to respond so quickly to our call."

The second man walked up, "I'm Senator Edwards, we're so pleased that you decided to join us on such short notice. And this is the Chairman of the Democratic committee, Steven Forger, as I'm sure you know." They all shook hands, smiled and then critiqued each other quickly with a single glance, a skill every good conspirator develops if they want to survive for very long. Self-preservation is always the first rule of staying alive politically.

"What a prodigious meeting, "the Governor blurted out, more out of nervousness than cordiality.

"Yes, we think it is," said Senator Edward, "we also have our speech writer with us, Joshua T. Potter, he had to become a speech writer just to explain his name, but he's a word-musician. He can make words weep or laugh." They all laughed while Joshua gave that look of, this is old material, lets move on. They all made their way to the fifth level and entered the Webster suite, which had all the amenities you would expect for distinguished guests.

"You must be wondering why we called you to such a secretive meeting, we're sorry for all this cloak and dagger but once you hear what we have to say, or ask, to be more precise, you'll understand why we have to go to such lengths," spoke Senator Colin.

"We have actually been watching you for some time now, Governor, and we like what we see," said Steven. "Your reputation has impressed many senators and congressman over these past 10 years. You've managed to stay away from scandals, you resurrected your State from a fiscal nightmare and revitalized several city centers, which the papers called a modern day renaissance. Plus you have become a national figure through the talk shows, Face the Nation and Meet the Press, that you've been on. Your not thinking of going to Hollywood are you?" Everybody laughed, but it was more out of relief than humor.

The Chairman continued, "And on the Today Show you came across as a family man, which has kept the conservatives happy. How have you managed all this?"

There was silence as the Governor was beginning to put the pieces together in his mind as to where this was going, he was overwhelmed, excited and was desperately trying not to let his imagination run ahead of the possibilities. "I would have to say, with careful planning and a lot of luck."

Everybody chuckled, because they all knew how true the Governor's statement was. A person's political life hangs on a thread and if just one wrong word is overheard in a conversation, then all it takes is one disgruntled person with a pen or newspaper to ruin your career.

"Yes, we were intrigued by the article in Life magazine that came out several months ago, called, 'A New Modern Political Maverick." Said Senator Edward.

Then senator Edward leaned forward while Chairman Steven Forger, senator Colin and Joshua all became serious, and said, "we're here to make you an official offer, actually it's the holy grail of politics, but there is a price tag that goes along with it, we want to be clear about that, but the rewards far outweigh the price. At least that's our feeling on the subject."

The Chairman spoke up, "We would like you to run for the Presidency eight years from now."

The world stopped, and the Governor felt like he was Alice in Wonderland or Buck Rogers being suspended in animation, or even Superman on an alien planet. Everybody looked at each other as the silence continued until the Governor said, "What an honor! I do have political ambitions, but the presidency was only a dream for me." His thoughts were rolling over in his mind like a child playing with marbles in his hands. He was struggling to keep his composure at this moment knowing they were watching his every move for signs of weakness.

"It's obvious that there is much work to be done. You're running for senator this autumn, we can help you with that. We know you already have a solid campaign going. We want you to start thinking of the presidency now, so by the time your second term as senator comes around, the word is out on the streets that you're a serious contender for the hope of this nation. That's if you're ready to be a party person, a team player…and someone who will do whatever it takes to go the distance," Senator Colin said with authority in his voice.

"I didn't get where I am today by myself, it takes people of influence, money and power to reach the top, and if you are the ones who have that kind of clout, then I'm the type of man who will play ball with you," the Governor said with delight and confidence. "You are offering to be my eminence grise behind the presidency."

"We see you understand perfectly." Said Steven.

Joshua spoke up for the first time, "they asked me to come along because my family is known for it's political conservative values throughout the Midwest, so I can help you connect with Middle America values. You wouldn't mind if I do some editing of your speeches and make a few suggestions that could broaden your appeal? You could *Univac them to us , we'll give you an encryption code, then I would send them back within a few hours ."

The Governor replied, "our office is not that advanced yet, can you supply one for us?"

"Sure, and this will keep our communication private and in-house." Joshua answered.

The Governor went on, "I believe in rhetoric, it's the music of the soul for our kind, sure, if it will get me more votes." .

The chairman added, "As you know, the democratic party has been slowly haemorrhaging due to a series of scandals. And President Eisenhower was elected because of his war record and they think he can still keep them safe from the Communism, and nuclear holocaust. So now what we're looking for is some alchemy, where we can pour all these problems into a sieve and they come our out looking like gold. And we believe you're part of that alchemist team that can make it happen because the people like you, you're a natural on television."

The Governor responded, "I've never relied on magic for my success, but I'm well aware that there is a thin veneer between truth and reality. And with some help from Joshua T. Potter, your spin doctors and image consultant, I believe we can turn the tide of public perception. After all, black is a very dark shade of white for us politicians.

The conversation, planning, strategizing, eating, drinking, scheming and the occasional congratulatory compliments went on into the early hours of the morning. They talked about Sputnik, the Space race, UFO's, the Suez

6

Canal, Communism, Civil Rights, Apartheid, and the Cold War. By the end the Governor needed a Bromo Seltzer* to settle his stomach.

It was a long black night for Jim and Andy on the roof across the street, as well as the drivers and other special branch men and women in the halls and rooms. But for the Governor, it was a moment, a flash, a thought that left him exhilarated, ecstatic and power hungry. He was going to speak to the world and for the world; he was going to be 'The President.'

As they reached the lobby, senator Edward stopped the Governor, grabbed his arm, turned him toward him and said; "now all of this is contingent upon a caveat, that you and your family stay free from any scandal, they're our number one nemesis. To quote from my high school drama class, 'The people are like water and the ruler a boat. Water can support a boat or overturn it.' [1] We can't afford to invest this heavily into your future just to start all over again with someone else. We're counting on you, just keep doing what you have been doing and the world will be yours, do I have your assurance on this matter?"

"Absolutely, don't give it another thought," the Governor said.

"If you run into any trouble, no matter how small it is, call us, we have influence country wide in many sectors of society. We're your friends, we're partners now, what concerns you concerns us, your enemies are our enemies and your friends are our friends, from this night forward we're cloned, married, there are no secrets between us now. Don't let us find out from some other source about a problem, we want to hear it from you. We're friends, you can trust us, understand?"

"Absolutely, friends, cloned, no secrets, together we'll win." The Governor responded.

"Your daughter Catherine, she's in her first year of university, you can depend on her?" Edward said with piercing eyes.

---

[1] William Shakespeare

"Of course, she's not only a politician's daughter, she's as ambitious as I am. She likes having a good time but she's not easily swayed by the under achievers." The Governor said reassuringly.

Edward moved closer to this ear and said in a quite tone, "we would like to assign a few special branch people to you and your daughter, very causal mind you. They would keep their distance and be very discreet. Once we begin to build our circle of influence concerning the possibility of you running in 8 years, we wouldn't know what opposition we may run into. Would that be OK with you?"

"I would be honored by your concern. And when you say special branch, what branch is that?" The Governor asked.

The kind of branch that very few people know about, you'll be briefed all in good time, but for now there just special branch. Edward's responded enjoying the intrigue.

"We'll assign a younger woman to your daughter, someone who can blend in with the college scene. You can discuss this with your wife of course, but let's keep this information from your daughter for now, she's young and we don't want any distractions at this time, it would be fatal to your future and to our parties' future." Edward's said all of this with one of those Mona Lisa smiles. The Governor could tell that he wasn't telling him all the truth; special branch personnel meant intrusion, ease dropping and tapped phones. Suddenly he realized how much his world was going to change. The Governor felt like a spotlight was shinning on his soul, and it wasn't love that was piercing his political exterior, it was fear.

They all *spilt , got into their cars and it was as if it never happened. The ride home was suddenly lonely, empty. It's the same kind of let down you have after eating a large amount of dessert, sweet to the taste, comforting to the stomach but depressing to the body. What was his wife going to say? How was he going to keep this a secret for so long? Could he trust these men and what kind of bed did he just climb into? It was all so surreal, he needed to get some sleep and have time to think it all through, something he should have done rather then say yes so quickly. But who could resist such an offer, was there any man or women who could walk away from such a gift, not him. This was the prize of a lifetime, of 100 lifetimes. No, he could have never said no, that's why he was where he was, because he did have the ambition, passion and drive. They were all good words, but he could sense those words were covering up the underlying reason – greed! And they knew he couldn't say no, which is one of the reasons they chose him. They knew him, and he didn't know them. They were the ones in control and not him. In thinking he had won the first round actually caused him to lose it. His yes was already a forgone conclusion, all the pomp and circumstance was only a smoke screen for their own political means, now he was going to have to figure out how to get what he wanted without selling his soul. The schemer had been scammed, the con man had been conned. And it was all too easy for them.

He drove home just as the sun was dawning; it was dark yet light, just like this situation. He wanted to shout it to the world, but fear was stifling his joy. What had he gotten his wife and Catherine into? So much power in the office of the Presidency, yet he felt controlled, hemmed in, not his own person. So much influence yet being so influenced. It was going to be a tight rope, the elation of scaling the heights while fearing how far one could fall. This is going to call for a whole new level of cunning and courage.

The Governor woke up late that morning, his daughter had already left for University and his wife was at a local charity fund raiser for United Cerebral Palsy. The events of last night seemed like Science Fiction Theatre , real yet fictional. Emotionally he was a Vesuvius about to explode with excitement, but mentally, the intricacies of becoming president in 8 years was radioactive . However, all his dreams, all his planning and scheming, all his drive was paying off, he had been scouted and not found wanting. The future and the world was his!

# CHAPTER 2

# JESSE, THE UNASSUMING STUDENT

*"But God has chosen the foolish things of the world to put to shame the wise, and God has chosen the weak things of the world to put to shame the things which are mighty;"*

*1 Corinthians 1:27 NKJV*

Jesse entered Danton University late because his sister wouldn't share the bathroom, again. His sister had been sucked into the black hole of teenage life and could no longer make up her mind about anything, especially what to ware. She had become impossible to reason with. She had become craze about Jerry Lee Lewis, bobby socks and sliced bread.

As Jesse trotted down the hall he saw Catherine walking towards him, the former Class Valedictorian from his high school. Her hair was long and blonde, cascading, flowing as in slow motion and her skin looked *crazy . Just seeing her was like the warmth of the California sun on your skin. Her eyes were emerald green, and her classic British chiseled nose was right out of Hollywood. She had an intellectual elegance about her. And there she goes walking past me just like every other day, carrying her Hermes bag , in her fashionable clothes, looking *fab.

In his head he knew she would never notice him, but his heart dreamed. Each time she passed, he had a moral dilemma, their values were worlds apart, and their beliefs were gods apart. He had considered her gods a thousand times: the god of popularity, the god of power, the god of cool, the god of envy, the god of fashion. Her gods seemed to give her everything, or was it just her dad, who was the money and power behind her force. Her dad, the Governor was the former high school football captain as well as the captain of the team in university. He led both Danton High and the Danton University teams to victory years ago... and today everybody still loved him.

And then there's...me, Jesse. Everybody knows my type from High School, that *cube student slipping through school unnoticed. The wallflower who is uncool, unsung, and not even as popular as the *nerds . But, actually, I'm smart, a nice guy, and I've been told I'm "good-looking" by someone other than my mom, and I'd like to think I'm funnier than the frats who sat at the University cafe chugging down drinks. And why am I so unpopular? Because to the average student Jesus means no sex, no drugs, no beer, no pranking teachers or students, no good movies, no dumping girls because you found another one better than the one you're dating, and always telling your parents the truth. That's Stone Age living. If you had to choose between Jesus and self, it's a no brainier: self wins every time.

So we live in different worlds. She's front-page news and I'm the back cover. But hey, it's not all bad; I'm eighteen and loved by my parents. I don't need popularity. I would like it, but I don't need it. But most of all, I've experienced genuine forgiveness. I know I've been branded a Pilgrim because they consider me an anachronism, a person born out of time. My beliefs just didn't fit into this secular world any more. Who wants to be friends with their parents, who even thinks they need forgiveness, and right and wrong are archaic concepts. So many believe that having religious values is an enemy of pluralism. But, I'm content and secure, I would like to hang out with more people than my parents, but my relationship with God is just too important to sacrifice for a pretty face or acceptance by the crowd.

Jesse finished his last class and ran for the door. He thought, "I have to find a ride home, it's raining like cats and dogs outside." Jesse ran outside and spotted Nick, his best friend since middle school when they dissected a frog together in eighth-grade science. They had both dared each other to drink the formaldehyde, and when they threw up simultaneously, they were forever bonded. From there it was one practical joke after another, summer camp with their church youth group and late night studying together. Nick was a *jet, but he was the kind of person that could get lost in a phone booth.

Nick was running toward the parking lot with his jacket pulled over his head to keep the rain off. Jesse caught up to him quickly.

" Nick, can I catch a ride home?" Nick turned toward him.

"Yeah, yeah. I was looking for you inside. I wanted you to ride with me anyway, because look." Nick pointed at a Chevrolet Corvette that looked brand-new..

Jesse squinted in the rain. "Fab!" *

Nick smiled. "Yeah. I scored*, man."

Jesse gave Nick a quizzical look as the two of them opened the doors and got inside.

"My Dad just bought it. I get to drive it as long as I keep my grades up, he knows I'm a genius."

"Cool ride," Jesse replied, "This is the one with the power glide automatic transmission and a 290 hp engine, *nifty."! As they started riding around Jesse thought. With a ride like this, I might just get a glance from Catherine

Jesse's house was your typical New England Cape, white with black shutters and window boxes bursting with purple pansies, a small, inviting porch in the front and in the backyard—a favourite spot when he was a child - a swing that he and his dad built together when he was only six. He had played, imagined, flown, sang and talked to God on many Saturdays. It was a house that said, "a family lives here" a house that embraced you as you walked up the pathway. It got smaller as the family grew, first Jesse and then his sister Amy, but it was home in every sense of the word. Jesse knew some kids whose parents had been divorced so they couldn't tell who their real cousins or uncles were any more. And there were other kids whose parents gave them everything but love. If parents could only hear their kids talking in the cafeteria at University, they would either die of shame or cry in disbelief. Jesse had his challenges with his parents but, after eighteen years, they were his friends as well as his mom and dad.

"Thanks for the ride. You really do have it *made in the shade Nick with this *chariot, I'll be taking advantage of this every day till you mess up," Jesse said as he grabbed his books and got out of the Corvette . "See yah." He walked up the pathway and reached for the front door when his sister, Amy, came bouncing out like Tigger in Winnie the Pooh, "gosh Jesse!" She cried. "You scared me!"

"You almost broke my tooth with the door!" Jesse said. "What's the rush? "

"It's Friday," Amy shouted, "I'm off to a sleepover at Linda's house, cool people actually do things on Friday nights! See yah."

Was I that goofy at thirteen? Jesse thought. Or am I becoming like my parents? Scary. He dreaded the thought. He paused for a moment in the front hall; genuinely appreciating the familiar smell of his mother's cooking. He threw his books down and called," I'm home, Mom!" as he walked into the kitchen.

His mother said, "Hi, sweetie. How was collage?"

"O, besides the peer pressure, drug dealers, communist front league and the student anarchists, it was the same old same old, except Nick gave me a ride home in his father's new Corvette . Whitewall tires, sports coup, *flip top, and fast, what a *neat *chariot. …."

" Huh," his mom said. She began chopping some carrots. " Nice to see his dad has his priorities straight."

Jesse responded. " What do you think? We sell the house and get the same car?"

"I'll give it some serious thought in my next life," she answered. Jesse decided to push the point a little further.

"If I had that kind of car, I might be able to actually attract a girl. You know it would be a perfect incentive to motivate me toward excellence."

"Well, let's hope you are able to find a girl who likes you for who you are and not what you drive," his mom interrupted. "Your time will come. Just look at it this way: your heart is being spared all those flings that last for a nano second and end with, 'I've found someone better.' This way, you won't be carrying any of those hurts into your one true relationship. I wish I had been so fortunate."

"How am I going to have one true love if I don't even have one to start with?" His mother stopped cutting the carrots and looked at him. She smiled. "God has a plan for you Jesse, and for your life, and when that moment comes you will know who your one true love is."

Jesse thought, *such a cop-out. That's always your fail-safe answer. How can I argue with God's plan?* His mother interrupted Jesse's thoughts as if she knew what he was thinking, "it's not just God's plan, you're in on it too."

Jesse answered, "I think it's God's plan for me to go to Nick's party next Friday night, that OK with you? Everybody's having parties everywhere because it's the end of exams." He hadn't been to many parties, not because he hadn't been invited, but it would always end up in another moral dilemma. However, this party would be different. " His parents have even hired bouncers to make sure things don't get out of hand. I may even sleep over if it's gets to late."

"Are you hoping Catherine will be there?" His mom asked

"How do you know about Catherine?" Jesse asked with surprise

"I heard you mention her name when you and Nick were playing basketball out front last week." His mom said with a smile.

"I doubt it, I don't think it would be good for her Dad's image, coming to a party with mere mortals, and besides, Catherine and her dad would think we were the Christian national party because most of Nicks friends are Christians. As the daughter of the Governor and former Mayor of Danton she has a certain decorum to keep, and from what I can tell, he never let's her forget it. He's a Politician first and last, and she's a carbon copy. "

Jesse's mom looked unsettled, " You mean she's immoral."

"No, Jesse spoke quickly, more like amoral."

"I thought she came to church with you some years ago?"

14

"She did, and she even made a commitment, but I think the pressure of political life has strangled any spiritual life out of her." Jesse said sadly

"You have another moral dilemma on your hands again?" His mom answered.

"When do I not have a moral dilemma, finding true love in a world of relativism seems like the impossible dream."

"It is impossible if you settle for less than God's best, but if you trust God than miracles can happen!" She said with concern and confidence. "I'll let Dad know about the party when he gets home just to make sure he hasn't made any other plans." His mom said. "And just to let you know, your dad has been having some irregular heartbeats and is at the hospital right now having some tests done. The doctor doesn't think it was serious but they wanted to be safe rather than sorry so they ordered a battery of tests for him. Pray for him, would you?"

"Absolutely, mom." Jesse ran upstairs.

Dad seemed fine when he came home that evening and he was cool with the party. He wouldn't have interfered but he did like being informed. The party was a good distraction for Jesse, he had a lot on his mind and some relief from real life issues that he was working through was welcomed. His mom's words just kept coming back to him about how he would know when he found the right girl. Maybe he was rushing it a little, but he couldn't wait. Eighteen years seemed like a long time for him to find the girl of his dreams. Keeping busy with school, sports and church activities was growing thin.

The seconds seemed to stretch into hours when he thought of the party. It was going to be huge, the last big bash* of the school year. Nick's dad was like the J.Paul Getty of Danville , and his house was crazy. His parties were always *swell.

The day before the event, he helped Nick get everything ready, like ordering food, hiding breakables, and cleaning the pool. Jesse was so excited he didn't mind the work. And finally, Friday night came. People began filing in around eight, and by ten the party was *buzzing . It was cool to be around, but there was no Catherine. He was kidding himself to think she would come to Nick's party.

"Jesse, you've been picking at that dip for like thirty minutes." Nick said. He looked crazy, wearing a button-down shirt, high waisted jeans and slip on shoes . It looked like he had just walked out of a fashion magazine. Jesse stopped playing with the food. "So, did the whole year turn up?" he asked.

"Everybody but Catherine." Nick replied, "The gods are not allowed to mingle with mortals." "That's just *peachy ," Jesse answered. "Well, I may as well make this a perfect, dateless school year. That way, if I just have one date in college, it will be a one hundred percent improvement."

# CHAPTER 3

# CATHERINE, A VICTIM OF POPULARITY

*"There is a way that seems right to a man, But its end is the way of death."*

*Proverbs. 14:12 NKJV*

"I'm off to the bash* Daddy , I won't be home until very late." Catherine yelled out from the top of the stairs.

Her dad the Governor came out of his office and looked up from the bottom of the stairs, "I know you know this but please don't do anything that you will regret or will embarrass us. You know how those newspapers just love to crucify us over the smallest thing. You remember the photographs of you in your bathing suit falling into the pool after having too much to drink. I had to do some damage control with the police on that one. You and everybody else were underage at that party."

"Ever since you came home from that meeting you had last week, the one you have never talked about, you've been edgy. And now your going all-protective on me, is there something I should know about?" Catherine replied

"In this family we all have a symbiotic relationship, what's good for one is good for all, and what's bad for one is bad for all. I'm not being over protective, I'm parenting and protecting our good name. You do remember whose head of this house don't you?" Her dad stated indubitably.

Mom came out of the living room reading to herself from her latest Harper's magazine and looking up said, "Oh hon, you know Catherine, she's as politically minded as we are. She'll be careful, but we also need to let her be 18 and have some fun, you do remember having fun don't you Stan. Why, when we were dating we went to the state fair...."

"Let's not bring up ancient history, we have to deal with the here and now, OK Cat, just remember you're a "Stone" when you're having fun, that's all I ask, decorum is the order of the day." Dad reiterated. "And by the way, that meeting was just another campaign strategizing *chinwag about my running for state senator." He said with a controlled tone.

"And another thing, you and mom have been talking a lot, not that it's a bad thing but it's definitely different, kind of sweet, but it's not you dad, so what's going on? You know I'm going to find out so its better you tell me then some newspaper." Catherine said authoritatively.

"I will tell you Cath, but now is not the right time. I will tell you this, its good news."

"I gathered that, you and mom have been acting like little school kids again, singing, happy and more cheerful than ever. You're not pregnant are you?" Catherine replied.

"Absolutely not, you've been our pride and joy Cath. And besides, we don't want to start all over again." Her mom replied.

"OK, off with you, we can't have you missing the party of the year now, can we". Her dad said with relief.

When Catherine drove out of her driveway she noticed an unusual black Chrysler parked near their home that she had never seen before. It caught her eye because it was parked on the street, and nobody parks on her street because it's not polite. All the neighbors have this unspoken rule to keep the street looking exclusive.

Across town on Salisbury Street, Catherine and her entourage arrived at the party hosted by Hanna Horton, she was one of the supreme rulers in their high school days. This *bash was filled with the Ivy leagued, *Frat boys, even some postgraduates, the beautiful people and the ones who could buy their way in and be tolerated by the takers. Since it was the last party of the year everything was a dare. How many beers could you drink in 10 minutes? How long could you kiss one person? Who could you manage to sleep with? Who would have the guts to do the hard drugs? The party was going *gangbusters and Catherine, the envy of every girl, was surrounded by the frat boys who were giving her shot after shot of alcohol in the hopes of getting her *loaded .

The girls were pushing the guys into the pool, the outdoor sauna was filled with bodies and edged by beer bottles while the clubhouse was throbbing with rock music and dancing. Shirts and tops were coming off everywhere, voices were getting louder and more and more bodies were lying down on the grass, chairs, couches and inflatables. And the only adults on the premises were the bar tenders.

By the end of the night Catherine found herself with Ted Barlow because of his add-nauseam pestering. He was the tight end on the football team and very popular with the cheer leading team, (if you know what I mean). In Catherine's eyes Ted was the type of guy who was aspiring to mediocrity. It was confirmed by the misspelled tattoo on his upper right arm which read, 'regret nohing.' Being the hero of the college football team was his life ambition. He "rescued" Catherine from the frat boys, making a big show of telling everybody that he would be looking out for her, only to get her alone behind the oversized couch in the family room. First they were laughing at each other's slurred speech, then they were *necking , until Ted became physically pushy. He wanted more, and Catherine, desperate to preserve her cool, was all too willing to do whatever it took to make him happy - and keep him from *shafting her name.

Across town, in another world, Jesse sipped a soda while looking out of a window at the summer stars. *I wonder if Catherine is having a peachy* time? Of course she is, she's the life of any party. I have got to get her out of my head, my life is so prosaic compared to hers. There's just no middle ground, unless I become schizoid and live in two worlds again.*

Jesse's mind went back to his junior year in High School when he went on a short term mission trip to England for the summer. He tried to live in two worlds during the ministry trip and what a disaster that was. He was so full of faith and purpose when he left for Great Britain but how things quickly changed once they started ministering in London. He was totally jet lagged, and the schedule so demanding that he couldn't drink enough coffee to keep himself going. Until he got to know Paul. Who would have thought a drug pusher would come on a mission trip. Jesse had never even heard of barbiturates because being a Christian one can live a sheltered and insular life.

He could remember the conversation between Paul and himself. Paul told him that the barbiturate wasn't even a drug, but more like a pharmaceutical stimulant. Not much different than drinking several cups of Camomile tea to relax you. Brain food was his exact words. It had become the study pills on university campuses. And it was so cheap, how could it have been a real drug at that price. It even looked like medicine. Jesse knew in his heart that it was a drug but the headiness of being in London, the peer pressure of appearing spiritual and wanting to impress the pastor's daughter seemed to lull his conscious to sleep. His proclivity was overridden with need. So he tried it. And oh did it work. He was sleeping fine and, his mind was focused again. He became the life of the mission trip.

How amazing, here he was performing dramas about the death and resurrection of Jesus Christ in Leister Square, worshipping God in Trafalgar Square and speaking about freedom from sin at Hyde Park Speaker's Corner while on drugs. How could he have been so deceived? The moral conviction grew and everyday he felt more like a hypocrite. He even tried to hit on the pastor's daughter in the church of Saint Martin's in the Field Church. How embarrassing. It wasn't who he was, it wasn't how he was raised and it wasn't what he believed.

As Jesse stood there looking out of Nick's window he could still recall the chronic fatigue he felt when he stopped taking the barbiturates. He had a hard time quitting once he got home, it took him over six months to finally let go of it. He had to lie to his parents, his sister Amy, the youth pastor and everybody who supported him through finances and prayer on the mission trip. He was a fake, a wolf in sheep's clothing, a con artist giving everybody a *snow job, and with every sermon he heard it just put the knife in deeper.

Jesse finally surrendered one night with his youth pastor, they prayed, he repented and he shared his sin, yes, he had to admit that it was sin. Sin to himself, to God and to his parents. That was the hardest thing, to see the disappointment in their eyes. They forgave, they embraced and the relationship was restored, but Jesse never wanted to go through that again. He spent the next three months biking every weekend to clear his head. He was a bit of an adrenaline junky and it made him feel alive again after his near soul death. Cycling was Jesse's Neverland, all he had to do was point his bike toward the North Star and fly away. No, living in two worlds was like having a multiple personality, and he vowed never to displease God like that again.

# CHAPTER 4

# THE PAST IS RESURRECTED

*"But the inhabitants of Gibeon… worked craftily, and went and pretended to be ambassadors. And they took old sacks on their donkeys, old wineskins torn and mended, old and patched sandals on their feet, and old garments on themselves; and all the bread of their provision was dry and moldy. 6 And they went to Joshua… and said to him and to the men of Israel, "We have come from a far country; make a covenant with us."*

*Joshua 9:3-15 NKJV*

Catherine didn't get up till noon, and once she felt her head, she wished she hadn't woken up at all, the nauseousness in her stomach, the abundance of alcohol from last night and not enough food all made her feel revolting*. *What happened, I feel like I've had a \*knuckle sandwich?* She thought, as the whole night seemed like a blur. *I remember the drinking, the dancing, the incredible loud music and guys swarming me and, O, Ted! Why on earth did I end up with Ted, he's such a \*bootlegger . This could be embarrassing if he decides to make me one of his trophies and tells all his teammates.*

Catherine staggered into the bathroom and splashed warm water on her face. She looked into the mirror and thought, *so this is what being \*Queen looks like, Ugh! Was Ted a cheap or an expensive date for maintaining the enviable position of popularity? I suppose my dad could answer that question, he knows all about winning through compromise. This looks ugly, not beautiful; I feel empty, not heroic. I must be an amateur to be having thoughts like this, my dad never seems unsure of himself. How does he do it?*

It was one o'clock and they were all sitting down for lunch. The food didn't look appetizing but Catherine knew she needed something on her stomach to settle it.

"You feeling OK honey?" her mom asked.

"No, I feel the way I look." Catherine grunted.

Her dad brought her a coffee to help kick start her day, "your a knight in shining armor dad." Catherine mentioned.

"It takes years to become a pro at parties, the trick of the trade is to look like your drinking a lot, having a great time, but not consuming very much and taking care of business. It's taken mom and I years to perfect our act." Her dad said with pride. "You didn't embarrass us last night, did you?"

"I can hardly remember last night.' Catherine said with disgust.

"Well, let's hope nobody else does either." The Governor boomed as he got up from the table. "I'll have to invite you to more of my parties to teach you the ropes, and as a matter of fact, were going to Washington D.C. in a few weeks."

"Washington, Dad, now you have to tell me what's going on, all night meetings, Washington D.C., sit back down and tell me what you and mom have been smiling about all week."

"This is big news Catherine, and I don't know how to prepare you for it other than just say it. The meeting I had last week was with the National Democratic party, the leader of the house, some senators and their speechwriter. Plus there were special branch men and women everywhere. It felt like a political fiction novel.

"Were the special branch guys good looking, daddy?" Catherine inquired.

"No, but you don't need to concern yourself with them, its mom and I that they're interested in." Her dad said quickly.

"You're no fun daddy." Catherine said smiling.

"I wasn't aware of it, but the Democratic Party has been watching me and the development of my career. And they see me as one of their best frontrunners, which means they're going to put their weight and influence behind me in the race for State Senator. Do you know what this means, their going to help us fundraise, and they know everybody. Plus their letting me have access to one of their top speechwriters. This is it, we're going to win this race."

"Don't let it go to your head daddy." Catherine said shyly.

"Don't let it go to my head, it went to my head before you were conceived. I was born for this, this is my fate, my destiny, my purpose in life. And it's all happening. Now you know why I said what I said last night."

"What was that?" Catherine responded queasily.

"About not doing anything that would embarrass us. It's more important than ever now. I've told you over the years that there is nothing worse than a scandal to stop a political career." Her dad said with firmness.

"Don't worry Daddy, I enjoy the power base just as much as you do, it has its advantages. I'm your daughter and I'll ride this horse all the way to the capital if that's where you want to go." Catherine said sheepishly. Catherine then looked over at her mom and the two of them agreed with an amused smile and a nod of their heads.

"Don't get ahead of yourself, we're talking about the Senate race." Her dad said.

"As long as we're all happy, that's all that matters." The mom chimed in.

"Right, hon, I believe we're all happy." Catherine's dad replied

All of a sudden Catherine and her mom looked at each other and had the same thought, then they looked at Stan. "We're going to need some new dresses for this special occasion." They said in unison.

"I can see that I'm going to have to add a special family social slush fund to my campaign budget." Stan said with a look of amusement.

"This party is in two weeks so I suggest you and mom go to the Macy's and find something suitable to wear. It's black tie for me and formal dress for you ladies."

"This means the whole ensemble mom, the dress, shoes, purse, *parure and elbow length gloves. Shell we do Christian Dior, Coco Chanel, Mary Quant or Elsa Schiaparelli , or maybe even May Vogue ? Catherine said with a beaming smile.

"I'm sure we'll find something that will bring out the best in all of us. It's been awhile since we've been to Washington D.C. But it's an enthralling city. The last time we were there we were entertained at the Hay-Adams Hotel. And it was enchanting. This will be a first for you Catherine and you're going to love it. Pennsylvania Avenue, eloquent venues, the Capital, hobnobbing with Senators, congressmen and women, intrigue, and if it's what I think it is, the President and the first lady may be there as well. It's going to be a glittering gala," Catherine's mom described.

Catherine and her mom left for Macy's and the Governor went to his offices downtown. He parked in his personal parking space and walked up the grand entrance to the Danton state building. It was an early 19th century government building built to impress. Six massive columns with the Roman emperors wreath carved at the top of each of them, and at the base were key Biblical inscriptions reinforcing the covenant the city made with God 250 years ago. And written above the entrance was, "Justice for all who enter this building." The Governor opened the large wooden carved door with its brass door handle to see his ombudsman waiting for him. He investigated the complaints against the government and he had that worried look on his face. This was not unusual behavior for Frank as he was fastidious about his responsibilities. But today his face filled the foyer with alarm.

"What's wrong Frank, you look like you've seen a ghost." The Governor said.

"I have Governor, remember the bookkeeper you fired six years ago for embezzling funds." Frank blurted out.

"Of course I do, and I was merciful because he should have gone to prison, it was only the scandal that saved him, and my good nature." The Governor proudly said.

"Well, he's back and sitting in your office lounge waiting for you, with a smile on his face." Frank said with concern in his voice.

"What does he want, Frank?" The Governor questioned.

"He wouldn't tell me except that he had some very valuable information that could help your chances for getting elected as Senator." Frank nervously replied.

The two of them were now walking with a quickened step, saying hello, waving, shaking hands with some of the staff. Then the Governor stopped and asked, "do you think he's trying to *shaft me with this information, or blackmail me to rehire him?"

"I don't know Governor, but he looks quite smug and cocky." Frank said worriedly.

"It's always the little foxes that spoil the vine, Frank." The Governor responded.

"What do you mean Governor?" Frank asked with confusion.

"Oh, it's nothing Frank, just something I heard a minister say when I attended a special service at the Lutheran church held in honour of my election to Governor years ago. His words may have been prophetic. Let's hope not Frank, let's meet this insignificant swindler and see if we can run him off again." The Governor boosted.

Frank and the Governor entered his suite of offices to first greet his secretary. She told him of Glenn, the former bookkeeper who was waiting for him. They walked over to Glenn and the Governor reached out his hand and said, "Glenn, what a surprise to see you around here again."

"It's an unexpected visit, I admit, but thanks for seeing me. I know this is awkward for both of us after what I did six years ago." Glenn said in an apologetic way.

"It's always best to be largess about these things, Glenn, let's go into my office and see what this is all about." The Governor boomed with his Cheshire smile.

The Governor sat behind his large and stately executive desk while Glenn and Frank sat down on well-cushioned club chairs. These chairs arrived their name from gentlemen's clubs where men sat around discussing politics, drinking and smoking cigars. It gave the Governor an air of respectability. Glenn had a large briefcase so it was good that the chairs were oversized.

"Now what's this all about Glenn, suddenly appearing after 6 years?" The

Governor asked.

"I still live in Danton as you may know, and I've been following your Senatorial race this past year. From all the polls I hear on the 6 O'clock news I'm aware that you're only 9 points in the lead.

"So you still take an interest in politics, do you now?" The Governor interrupted.

"Yes, that was the original reason I wanted to work for you when you were Mayor of Danton, I've always loved politics. You know, the intrigue, the potential of influence. I know I was only a bookkeeper but as I said in my interview, it was a stepping stone to greater aspirations. That was one of the reasons you hired me, you liked my gumption, I believe that was the word you used. Well, that's why I'm here today. Six years ago when I was doing your books, I noticed a discrepancy in the books over the land fill deal you had contracted with GreenEver corporation. I wanted to bring it to your attention but if you remember you were completely preoccupied with the unions who were on strike over garbage collection. And the public were breathing down your throat. In your panic you told the office to fix any of our own problems because you had more important things to do than doing our job for us." Glenn shared.

"I vaguely remember, the smell and public outcry I well remember, but this GreenEver corporation, isn't that owned by Senator Jackson, my political opponent? Yes, the first black Senator in this state who used his race card to play the victim and win." The Governor said with distance in his voice. "But I do admire his proletarian approach, he did successfully galvanize the racial issue and storm the gates of political whiteness."

"That's the one, Governor." Frank interjected.

"Well, that's why I'm here today Governor, because I may have some information about your incumbent Jackson that could help you win your Senatorial election." Glenn said shyly.

"Really?" The Governor said interested while he leaned forward in his chair. "You have my full attention, Glenn."

"Do you want me taking notes or recordings of this meeting Governor?" Frank asked.

"No, Frank, this is just a friendly chat between an old employee and his former boss." The Governor replied. "Go on Glenn."

"The reason I noticed this is because of the garbage strike. We were paying the GreenEver Corporation $105.40 per tonnage, which was contractual, but during the strike when they were not collecting the garbage they continued to charge us double the amount per tonnage for the entire 12 week period. And then when the strike was over, they increased their cost by $10,000.00 more each month for the remaining three years of their contract. This meant they overcharged us during those 3 months of the strike $442,680.00, and then if you add the additional $10,000.00 each month for the next three years you get an additional $360,000.00 but I was........dismissed so I never brought it to your attention again. ." Glenn related. "The amount was small in comparison to the overall budget and your accountant didn't seem concerned, they reported various surcharges to justify their charges but it was in violation of the contract."

"Are your suggesting that The GreenEver corporation committed fraud with our local government?" The Governor asked with wide eyes and a half smile.

"Well, I don't know if I could be the judge of that Governor, but I'm sure if your accountant goes back and looks at the contract and figures you'll discover the same thing I did. Concerning fraud, now that's up to the courts to decide. But I think it would be a news worthy item that could influence public opinion in your favor." Glenn said cautiously.

"So Glenn, why are you wanting to help me win when I'm the man who fired you?" The Governor asked pointedly. "And why now, why not 6 months ago?"

"You were considerably ahead of your opponent 6 months ago and I didn't think you would need me then, but now that the gap in the polls are closing I just thought this information could help you. Plus, I guess this is my way of doing penitence. I am sincerely sorry for what I did. I completely sabotaged my whole career and any political ambition I could have had." Glenn said remorsefully.

"Stan and Frank looked at each other and smiled. "You did right Glenn in coming to me, and I trust we can keep this matter confidential in the future as well?"

"I'm not going to make the same mistake twice Governor, I've learned my lesson." Glenn spoke emphatically.

"Yes, I believe you have." The Governor replied. "I'll have my accountant look into this matter and if we need any more information from you Glenn, my secretary will contact you. Please make sure you give her your current phone number so we can call you." The Governor told him.

"There is just one more thing Governor, and that is, I'm struggling financially right now. Is this kind of information valuable to you?" Glenn asked sheepishly.

"This kind of information is very valuable, and we deeply appreciate it because it could expose criminality and bring the tax payers justice, as well as let them see what kind of man they may be voting for. But, I can't pay you for this type of information, that would be illegal for me to use government funds for such a thing. We're not like newspapers who pay their informants. But I can do you a favor, which may help you in another way, how does that sound?" The Governor informed Glenn. "I'll let Frank and you talk about that on your way out, I know he will take care of you properly. Is that to your liking?"

"Thank you Governor, you have always been kind even when I cheated you." Glenn responded.

Frank and Glenn walked out, gave his secretary the needed information and then discussed the form of favor that would compensate Glenn for his help. Glenn and Frank shook hands, Frank walked back into the Governor's office and Glenn drove away in his used Ford .

As Glenn drove down the street he stopped at the first phone box. He opened his briefcase and inside of it was a tape recorder. He rewound it and listen to the tape. "Yes", Glenn shouted, "it worked." He got out of the car and make a call to Senator Jackson. Senator Jackson answered saying, "Is it done?"

"Yes, Senator Jackson, he reacted just the way you said he would and I have the whole conversation recorded on the Mohawk Midgetape recorder that you gave me. ." Glenn said with glee.

"My aide, Harry will rendezvous with you at 4, go to the north car park at Lake Mere and you can fill him in with the details. And Glenn," Jackson said,

"Yes." Glenn waited

"Good job, he'll have your money as well." Jackson said.

"Thanks, I've waited a long time for payback." Glenn stated.

Glenn was a toxic, beguiling individual, whatever relationships he had always ended up broken, like caustic form in the wake of a wave. But for him, he saw people only as stepping stones to some personal glory. And today, he felt an aura of glory beaming from his face. A crooked smiled formed on his face, his eyes squinted and he cranked his Frank Sinatra music up to sing at the top of his lungs as he drove towards his future. In this moment he was invincible. He had thought long and hard on how he could undermine the Governor and have his revenge. To Glenn, the Governor was a bloated toad, croaking pretentious nonsense and he had endured it for 3 years when he worked for him. But now he was rubbing shoulders with Senator Jackson and a potential presidential candidate. He believed this time he had hooked his wagon to the right star, and it wasn't going to burn out like the last one.

Glenn looked at his recorder and thought to himself, "from the outside the recorder looks so innocent, but on the inside it held a recording that determines people's futures. It's the perfect camouflage, like me, I looked meek and repentive but on the inside I've become the quintessential con artist. The Governor fell for the tete-a-tete routine. He has given me the *royal shaft for the last time. " He laughed out loud.

When Frank walked back into the Governor's office, his words boiled over with incredulity. "I don't trust that *fink any more now than when we fired him."

The Governor made a preemptive cringe before he answered, "I agree, this conspiracy theory is too convenient, but we need to decipher the political code here before we make a move."

"We both know that Glenn is not smart enough to imagine such a plot, he had to have some collaboration, and I think we both know who is really behind this - Jackson himself." Frank explained.

"I agree, I'll call my friends in Washington to see if they can get to the bottom of this. That will keep our hands clean. In the meantime, have our accountant look into this anyway and let's see if he has any theories." The Governor voiced.

# CHAPTER 5

# THE VISITORS

*"Humans are satisfied with whatever looks good; God probes for what is good."*

*Proverbs. 16:2 MB*

It had been three weeks since his Danton Grover Hotel rendezvous with destiny. He still had not shared the full news with Catherine yet, and was surprised by how nervous he was as the Washington contingency pulled up to his house.

"Hello Governor," said Colin, the Senator from Wisconsin. He was at their first meeting in the Danton Grover a few weeks ago.

"A pleasure to see you," the Governor's wife said. "Yes, what an honour to have you at our house." The Governor chimed in.

"Come in, come in, you must be tired after your trip." The wife voiced.

They all stepped into the foyer of the house and continued their introductions.

"And this is Joshua, you remember him, our speech writer. The one who makes the magic happen." Colin said.

"Yes, I'm looking forward to working with him." The Governor replied

"And this is Ted Wilson, he is going to be your behind the scenes campaign manager over the next 8 years." Colin said decisively.

"A pleasure I'm sure." The Governor replied.

"You may be wondering who these men and women are? They're special branch, we wanted you to get acquainted with them and what their job will be. Normally they're protecting international personalities and dignitaries but we have borrowed them for a few months because we want them to get

32

to know you, and we want you to know how things will work. That acceptable to you Governor?" Colin replied to the look on the couples face.

"Of course, our lives are an open book, and I'm sure you have already done your homework on us." The Governor retorted.

"And of course we have brought a photographer, Monet, she wanted to meet you, see your house and tour around your city to get some ideas on promoting you during the campaign. Image is everything, they say. Joshua spins the words and Monet paints the picture. They're both geniuses when it comes to shaping public opinion. They want to turn you into a demagogue." Colin claimed.

They all laughed as they entered the house and made their way to the Governor's study. His study was everything you would expect a study to look like. The words above the door into his office read "Carpe diem," seize the day. They were carved into a brass plate. Inside, the first thing you noticed were the mahogany built-in bookshelves from floor to ceiling on three walls with large windows running from chair rail height to the ceiling; a grand mahogany desk with laid-in leather, covered with globe bookends, a banker's lamp, double brass ink stand and a name plate. He had the classic Armillary Sphere globe with the interlocking brass rings and to impress, his private collection of first edition books. And of course framed pictures of famous football players with autographs. The Governor certainly knew how to get what he wanted.

Everybody sat down in lushly upholstered leather backed chairs that made one feel like a statesmen. The Governor sat behind his desk, the position of power and importance. He leaned back, the only chair that did, clasped his hands behind his head and said, "So, where do we begin?"

Ted started, "This is Olivia, she's the one who has been assigned to your daughter. As a matter of fact she has been keeping an eye on her for the past 3 days. We would like this to be as low profile as we can. We don't want newspapers or anyone for that matter to become inquisitive as to why your daughter has a bodyguard. As you can see, she's young, beautiful and should be able to fit into the collage scene easily. And again, it's only for a few months, just to keep an eye on your daughters social life and what her habits are."

"Yes, beautiful and smart, you could be competition for my daughter's social agenda." the Governor said snidely with a flirtatious smile.

Colin, Ted, Monet and the special branch team suddenly had a peek through the looking glass of the Governor's real personality. They unanimously saw his underbelly and didn't like what was revealed. He wasn't just thirsty for power but lecherous. Olivia was feeling a little uncomfortable and was hoping his daughter wasn't like him.

Olivia answered, "I have been profiled for this assignment Governor, and my interest is not in the campus' social life, my job is to keep your daughter safe, out of trouble and protect her from any potential characters who may want to use her to get to you. She is your only daughter, she's high profile and the apple of your eye. You can bet your life that power hungry people right now are plotting, scheming and strategizing on how to bring you down. And we want to be wherever we need to be to stop them. Your daughter is a major player in all of this."

"She's also the one who is going to connect you with the younger generation. She's already very active on campus with young people all over the state regarding your campaign for State Senator, and we want to capitalize on that and increase your influence through her." Ted stated

"I have no problem with my daughter being part of your detail of protection. She's 18 and makes most of her own decisions now. As far as I'm concerned, this is a win win. Now she will have invisible parents watching over her. I may even learn what she's up too as well." The Governor replied with a sporty smile on his face as he surveyed Olivia.

Andy, the special branch person who was on the roof top the evening the Governor met the Head of the Democratic Party, interrupted the awkward moment by saying, "Olivia, you need to be going because Catherine will be coming home soon."

Steven, the Democratic Chairman responded to the Governor's remark to Olivia, "We all know it takes a certain Machiavellian prowess to become president, but appearing a philanderer in public will only hurt our image. And that type of remark you made to Olivia will communicate just that."

The Governor stood up from his chair, put his hands on the top of his desk and leaned forward saying, "I was testing Olivia to see what metal she was made of and I'm a bit surprised she needed the rest of you to come to her aid. My daughter is a formidable personality and when she discovers she has a special branch protectorate, she will put her through the paces. Now, let's not jump to hasty conclusions about me just yet, there will be ample time for that." His remarks diffused the tension in the room a bit but Colin and Edward glanced at each other knowing a diverging tactic when they see it, and they were impressed again.

What Andy and Olivia didn't know was that Catherine and Hannah were driving towards her house in her pink convertible Thunderbird . Her home was not the largest in Danton but it was stately. It was built entirely out of fieldstone with leaded windows and several chimneys. Over the driveway were multiple stone aches covered by a brass roof. It had an English baronial look that transported you back to more idyllic romantic times. The regal property was accentuated by two ancient Cyprus trees and a stone wall surrounding the entire lawn and gardens. As the Governor it had the privacy and exclusivity needed to create the right image.

Catherine and Hanna were talking about the summer holiday and the possible scenarios of what they could do as they approached Catherine's house. Their history professor was sick so their class was canceled, which is why Catherine arrived home early. When Catherine was pulling into her driveway she noticed the black Chrysler she had seen before.

"Look, look, Hannah." Catherine interrupted.

"It's a woman, and she looks like a university student. I never would have believed a woman was driving that car. Have you seen her before?" Hannah remarked.

"She is young, looks like a model but has an athletic body. Kind of like the female spy in The Two-Headed Spy . She must be with all those other cars and people inside meeting with daddy. When she leaves we'll go inside and see who my dad is meeting with." Catherine remarked.

"You don't think she was visiting your mom?" Hannah asked

"No, I couldn't imagine my mom meeting with anyone that age driving a car like that, no, the classic car says to me it's my dad. Besides, my dad love's to flirt, and she's a perfect mark for him." Catherine said with regret in her voice. "I wonder..."

"What do you wonder?" Hannah's voice sparked up with curiosity. The possibility of gossip in Catherine's voice immediately pecked her interest.

"My father had a meeting several weeks ago about his campaign, and he's been cagey ever since, I wonder if this has something to do with that?" Catherine continued. "take a picture of her and we'll see if we can find her in any of the journals from Washington in the library later ."

Hannah chimed in, "I love this spy stuff. Maybe we should go to a pawn shop and see if we can buy some spy gear, like surveillance detectors and binoculars, or even some tracking devices and bugs to put on their clothes. You could even put some listening monitors in your dad's study, then you'll really know what's going on."

"Let's not get all dramatic Hannah, I'm only interested in this woman who seems to be everywhere I am. She's gone now, let's go inside and see who daddy is talking too." Catherine asserted.

They started getting out of the car when Catherine said, "wait a minute, get back in, quickly." They jumped back into the car and slouched down so just their eyes were above the steering wheel. They both had their *cheaters on to help with the disappearing act.

"Look at those two men outside the front door, there dressed like FBI agents, the ones you see in movies . I hope this is not another secret society." Catherine questioned.

"This is getting more interesting by the minute, what is your dad into? Do you think he has hired some bodyguards or security because of his campaign for Senator?"

"Possibly. There not the kind of bodyguards you see at the clubs, these two are sharp dressers and are in peak physical condition. They look more official, more government in their mannerisms." Catherine added.

The two men went back inside and Catherine and Hannah started for the front door again. "When we get inside, lets go into the living room because it's across from my dad's study, hopefully it won't be too long before whoever is in there comes out, than dad will have to introduce us to them."

"Good plan, it's always exciting being your friend Cat, always intrigue. Drama is attracted to you like vampires to blood." Hannah remarked.

But the meeting did go on. Inside Colin, Edwards, Steven, Joshua and Ted started their conversation with,"the 50's is being called the age of consensus because 90 percent of the American population agree on what is the American dream, and you fit that bill. You live in the suburbs, have a good family life, you daughter is in University and your a success. Your the epitome of everything Russia is not, and that is good for us." They went on discussing in more meticulous detail the final months of the Governor's run for Senator. They monologued about current affairs, who the key pundits were, potential debates, development of bipartisan cooperation, what the Governor thought about the Cold War, America's intervention of Lebanon, the launching of satellites, nuclear power plants, the world series and a whole range of moral minefields.

When they all came out of the study, the Washington team came to see that the Governor was a connoisseur of ambition. He had a natural chameleon propensity. They knew he loved power and prestige but they had underestimated his political prowess. Steven, the Chairman of the Democratic committee and Ted the Campaign Manager were talking outside in the hall of their need to keep the Governor's addiction to power under control.

By the time Catherine's dad had made all the introductions to her and Hannah it was already late. Hannah called Beth for a ride home, and she couldn't wait to develop the picture she took with her camera . On the way home Hannah and Beth were speculating and creating plot after plot about the woman and the two men at Catherine's house. It was Beth's specialty, script writing.

At the house Catherine did learn that the guests were all from Washington, and they were key politicians and bureaucrat's that ran the Democratic party. And that the men were special branch, but the woman she saw earlier with the Chrysler remained a mystery. One enigma was coming together, but the other one would have to wait.

Her dad could see from her face that she was putting the pieces together regarding the meeting he had weeks ago. He walked over to her, grabbed her arm, puller Catherine close to him and said, "I'll tell you what's going on tonight." Catherine retorted with a coy smile, "you better, or I might have to ask one of these nice special branch men." Than she walked away with a whimsical swagger to let her dad know she was going to be a player in this game.

Catherine's mom had had food fit for the gods catered in for the guests, Blackticks Blue Cheese and Walnut Soufflé, Goat Cheese and Sunblushed Tomato Tarts, Baked Cornish Game Hens, Lamb top Sirloin, Salmon en Croute, King prawn skewers marinated with lemon grass, Florentine soup, Tuscan vegetables, Mediterranean Vegetable Risotto, Stuffed Butternut Squash, Roasted Baby Potatoes and Creamy Mashed Potatoes with Cracked Black Pepper. This was complimented with Fennel and Orange Salad with Fresh Cranberries and Green Apples and Caesar Salad. The desserts consisted of Tiramisu Parfaits, Creme Brûlée, Baileys Irish Cream Cheesecake and Strawberry and White Chocolate Charlottes. All this was served with gourmet breads, sauces, condiments likes Roasted Vidalia Onions with Balsamic-Apricot Glaze, and a sumptuous amount of wine. The meal was presented with the Governors flare for grandiloquence and stateliness but he did note who drank the most for future opportunities of loose lips.

After the meal the guests retired to the Danton Grover Hotel, the hired catering staff cleaned up the dining room and kitchen while the Governor, his wife and Catherine went into the den to discuss the meaning behind all these meetings with the Washington guests. It was getting close to 9:30pm and as fascinating as the meal and company were, she wanted to know what this meeting was all about.

They relaxed into the sofa's while Stan assumed his customary stance in front of their Elizabethan styled fireplace. All he needed was a cigar to create the full imitation of Winston Churchill. It was his common theatrical deportment when emphasizing a winning argument. But before he began to tell Catherine about the Presidency he had a thought, *when you get to the top and you think your the puppet master, you see that you have strings tied to you and someone else is pulling them from above. There's always a price.* Then his mind came back to his daughter.

"As you have rightly guessed, your mother and I have been on cloud nine these past weeks because I have been offered the crème de la crème by the Democratic party, they have asked me to run for the presidency in eight years." Stan pronounced with childish glee. Catherine screamed, than she put her two hands on her face and remained motionless with her mouth wide open and her eyes fastened on her dad. Her mother leaned over putting her arm around her shoulders and said, "its OK dear, you can breath now." As Catherine glanced toward her mother their two sparkling smiles met, and her dad was wearing his proud smile, the smile that says he had just won his lifetime achievement.

"That's what all this hubbub is about, these meetings, the extravagant dinner, my caution to you on the eve of your party and even the special branch. Daughter, this is the big time, the Nobel Prize in politics and that is why everything we do from this day forward can make or break me, and us, in the future." Stan stated.

Her dad and mom went on and on dramatizing about the next eight years. The political connections, the travel, campaigning, fundraising, the involvement of media and various organizations. They droned on as Catherines life was being rewritten. Her attention was startled into focused when her dad said, "authenticity, that's what they saw in me, and us as a family I might add. That's one of the reasons they chose me, our scandal free family life and political success. It was the winning combination that has now put us in the spot light." Her dad shared delightfully. *The presidency,* Catherine thought, *that would make her a superstar, like a Hollywood actress. This was getting better and better.*

But little did Catherine know that an unknown culture was brewing in her Petri dish.

CHAPTER 6

# THE PROPHECY

*"Like a lamb taken to be slaughtered and like a sheep being sheared, he took it all in silence."*

*Isaiah.53:7 NIV*

It was a magnificent Sunday morning with stunning cumulus clouds, bright sunshine and a cool 78 degrees. Perfect for biking, which Jesse was intending to do after church today. Everyone in the family was getting ready to go to the 11am service. Jesse left early because he was playing drums in the worship team. He loved expressing his heart and praising God through the drums. It was a highlight of the week for him.

He took his own car so he could make a quick escape after the service to mount Reeves. He was meeting up with Nick, Bundle, Christopher and Daniel, his cycling buddies. Today they were going to brave the death drop, a slightly slanted cliff that challenged even the best of cyclists.

Christian Life Church was packed even at 10:30am because a guest speaker was ministering, Evangelist Mary Sutton. She had a strong prophetic gift so everybody wanted a personal word from God, except for those who were hiding some secret sin. They had strategically placed themselves in the back seats of the church hoping they would not get a shot off the bow that would embarrass them. Even though everybody already knew what they were into, they were the only ones living in this deluded world of hypocrisy. It was a world Jesse was all too familiar with in London, England. He couldn't judge them, he felt sorry for them knowing the struggle they had to deal with from time to time.

Jesse made his way to the platform to begin rehearsal but the worship leader told the team there were too many people in the sanctuary to practice.

"Let's go into the back room and spend some time praying before we start the service" the worship leader said.

In the back room as the team were praying, Nori said she had a word from the Lord, "I'm not sure what this means, but I'm sensing in my spirit the word suffering. I don't know if that means there are people in the congregation who are suffering or if that word is for someone in this room, or if it refers to someone who may suffer in the future, but regardless, let's pray that God will meet that person in their hour of need."

Getting words from the Lord was not unusual, but suffering, who wants a word like that Jesse thought. *"Hope she's not referring to me."*

The service was *cooking that morning, worship took off right from the first song. The presence of God was weighty and the people responded with excitement. It's like there was electricity in the air. Howard's prayer for the city, the election, and the country was compelling. The service came to a crescendo as people gave testimonies, Lynda did a gospel song and a presentation on missions was given, and then Mary was introduced.

She was a quiet speaker, not your typical charismatic minister, but the congregation was sitting on the edge of their seats as she spoke. She had a commanding presence, an authoritative prescient tone that only comes from a godly life and many hours spent in daily prayer. A holy hush had fallen on the people, a stark difference from the cranking praise just moments ago.

And then, unexpectedly, she looked directly at Jesse. She walked down from the platform and stood right in front of him. Because Jesse was on the worship team he and the whole team sat on the front row every Sunday so they could be called upon in a moments notice. Jesse could feel the whole church staring at him and he was nervous. Was there some sin in his life that she was going to reveal, like the London incident? Or was he going to be called into some ministry that he didn't want to do?

"God has chosen you, young man, to a Calvary path. You will be misunderstood by those closes to you, and criticized by people you thought cared for you. The Lord says, ' *"Like a lamb taken to be slaughtered and like a sheep being sheared, he took it all in silence.'* That's what he's asking of you, to suffer in silence and let God defend you. Your soul will die and be resurrected, you will fall and be raised by His right hand. You will only have His word and His Spirit to rely on, but His grace will be sufficient."

Then she turned around and walked back onto the platform and continued speaking. She was talking about the hardships and the joy the early disciples experienced as they spread the message of Christ throughout the known world but he was only thinking about the prophesy. And you can bet that nobody else in the congregation wanted a prophesy like that . After hearing what she said to him, they were happy she kept preaching. As a matter of fact, he was the only one that morning to receive a prophesy, and it was the talk of the whole church.

People came up to Jesse and told me him was chosen for a special task and that they were going to pray for him. He knew what that meant, they were overjoyed that he was the one and not them who was chosen. Did this mean martyrdom? Did this mean some horrible disease was to be suffered or was my future plans in jeopardy? There was one thing Jesse was sure of, he would never find a girl who would be interested in suffering with him. This is not what he was *keen for this morning.

After the service the pastor and Mary came up to Jesse and wanted to see him in the pastor's study. He felt like a little school kid being sent to the principal's office. When they walked in and the door was closed, Mary immediately started praying. She was pleading with God, making intercession for Jesse with compassion and power, as one who has confidence in God. Her words were filled with faith and soon the room filled with heaven. This women had power with God, something Jesse had never experienced before. She was a woman of spiritual substance. Her prayer was intimate, undaunted and holy. Soon Jesse was being touched by divine love as she continued to pray. God's agape love came like wave after wave after wave pouring over him, bathing his inner most being. His heart swelled and he thought he was going to be raptured. He had never encountered God like this before, it was eternal. He felt like he was in the throne room of God. He fell to his knees, lifted his hands in the air and praise cascaded out of his heart. He lost all consciousness of the pastor and Mary as he worshipped God. This love overwhelmed him in a deluge. In God's presence he instinctually understood why Jesus sacrificed himself for mankind, why someone would lay down his life for a friend, how a mother could love their handicap child. This love was beyond altruism, it was sacrifice with no thought of one's self. He saw humanities worth and value through God's eyes of love and Jesse was willing in that moment to give up everything for their salvation. This love was compelling, enthralling, all consuming, without compromise. How his mouth could be speaking praises and his mind comprehending his love at the same time was a mystery to Jesse?

When she stopped praying silence filled the office, unspoken truth was being spoken everywhere. All three of them had had an unexplainable encounter with God. Jesse sat back in his chair and was attempting to absorb the miracle. Then Mary said to Jesse, "I don't know exactly what God has chosen for you, but I do know it's a path that will bring redemption to many. The Calvary road is not easy, but it's the highest calling God can give to his people. When the moment comes and the path of suffering is set before you, remember, he has chosen you for such a time and He will be your strength and courage. Today's meeting with God was in preparation for what will happen in the future.

"None of us have any idea what this prophetic word means, but I want you to know, this door is always open to you Jesse, and you can talk to me anytime. You're not alone in this, we will be here to walk this through with you." The pastor remarked with concern in his voice.

"Thanks", Jesse said, "but this prophecy may not happen for years to come, I may not even live here when it comes to pass."

"I have a sense in my spirit that it won't be long Jesse, but the most important thing is that you prepare yourself for this by developing a strong devotional life. Stay in the Word of God, pray without ceasing and develop a fervent heart of thanksgiving. Learn the voice of the Holy Spirit and know your God. These are the things that will enable you to endure any trial and like the Apostle Paul, come out victorious."

"An hour ago I was an 19 year old just wanting to go biking, now I'm being called to join the ranks of the early disciples." Jesse said with an unsettled expression on his face.

"David, Gideon, Timothy, Joseph and Jesus were all called at an early age to change the world, and God was more than enough for them. When the call comes we all have a decision to make, to yield or run." The pastor said

"And we all know what happened to Jonah when he ran from God's call, a big fish got him. I don't know if that's much of a choice, living inside of a whale or taking my chances suffering on land?" Jesse said dryly.

"Prayer, that's the secret," Mary said, "because He will reveal his purposes to you as well as strengthen you for the task."

The Pastor prayed and they left the church building. He was sure his parents wanted to talk with him and find out what the pastor and Mary said, but he thought biking would help take his mind off of suffering. The talk would just have to wait until evening. As he got into this car and sat in front of the steering wheel, the overwhelming love of God permeated the car and Jesse's entire being. Tears poured from his eyes running down his cheeks as he sobbed uncontrollably. It was not because of sadness but he was ecstatic, his heart completely captivated to such a degree that all his concerns he had in the office about suffering and his future just dissolved. A grateful willingness flooded his mind and instead of fearing the future, he was actually anticipating it. The words that Jesus prayed in the garden before he was crucified floated into his mind, "not my will but yours be done." Through the looking glass of God's love he could now understand how Jesus could have prayed such a prayer. This love enabled him to comprehend the difference between his selfishness and God's transcendent love. They stood juxtaposed like good and evil, light and darkness, and he saw how he had spent his life trying to preserve his reputation and how most of his decisions were in self interest.

In this holy ecstasy he surrendered his life, his future, his plans and his preferences. He wanted this love to govern his actions, because he now knew it was the only force on earth that could bring purpose and meaning to mankind. How real this love was, "for God so loved the world, that he gave his only son...." This love was big enough for whatever Jesse had to face. Jesus poured out his life for all mankind. And that's what Jesse was to do now, in someway, give his life as well.

When he cleared his eyes he became cognizant of an luminous afterglow. Worship songs sprang from his heart as he drove off. *How a moment encounter with God can change one's life forever,* Jesse thought. No wonder King David said in the bible, "in your presence is the fullness of life, and at your side are pleasures evermore." Those words were no longer just a song he sang at church, but today he had been *clued in. He had met with God today!

Ps. 16:11 NIV

# CHAPTER 7

# THE POLITICAL VATICAN - WASHINGTON D.C.

*"'In the pride of your heart you say, 'I am a god; I sit on the throne of a god*
*in the heart of the seas.' But you are a man and not a god, though you think you are as wise as a god."*

*Ezekiel 28:2 NIV*

This was their prodigious night, like Cinderella the Stone's were attending the Democratic congressional ball at the Willard InterContinental Washington Hotel on Pennsylvania Avenue, built in 1847. Famous people like Henry Clay and Abraham Lincoln stayed there, and it was the same hotel they stayed at years ago to explore Washington.

The Governor, his wife and Catherine arrived in a limousine compliment of Senator Edwards. Before they stepped out of the car Stan said to Catherine, "now remember, carry each glass of champagne around for about an hour, take only very small slips because when it's about half empty every man will approach you to fill it for you. Look like your drinking but don't drink. All of us need to be about our wits tonight and not be enamored with the glamour and pomp."

They made their way out of the car and were escorted to the ballroom walking on a red carpet that began on the marble steps in front of the hotel. Both sides of the isle were lined with elegant flower arrangements, calla lilies, alstroemerias, cymbidium orchids, dahlias, stephanotises, tulips, peonies, hydrangeas and flowers shipped in from all over the world. And each arrangement had American flags in them. In-between them were security guards, hotel staff and waitresses serving champagne as guests walked in. It was an imposing entrance that made the Stone's feel like aristocrats.

They were greeted by Senator Edward, Steve Forger the chairman of the Democratic committee, Ted Wilson the campaign manager for the president and Senator Colin's. They, in turn, introduced them to each other. The ball was filled with senators, congressman, commissioners, the under secretary, members from the house of representatives, various state Governors, Cabinet members and judges, with a few supreme court judges. And besides them there were secret service everywhere and advisors from all governmental departments. It was the who's who of Washington. And of course the fundraisers, like giant leeches glad-handing the deep pockets and smooching the widows. Like financial artisans they painted a future of hope and glory to these people, and the people were more than happy to overpay for the fundraisers investment painting. Yes, Catherine had arrived, she felt at home like an eagle taking to flight. She was born for this. It was like the planets had aligned and the whole universe made sense.

Everybody at the party was talking about Sputnik, Russia's first manned space ship. Were they spying on us and how big was the communist threat to America. Others were concern with the Suez Canal. And on a lighter note they all knew the latest show of "I Love Lucy" and would they be caught on "Candid Camera"?

Joshua T. Potter, the speech writer, pulled the Governor aside and said, "we would like to do a piece on Catherine, as well as scatter some glossies of her college life across the pages of the Danton globe magazine. Do you think she would be open to that?

"She has already informed me that she's in this all the way, she's a chip of the old block." The Governor said smiling.

"Great, I'll have a conversation with her sometime tonight and make all the arrangements." Joshua replied.

The Governor made his way over to the Chairman of the Democratic Party, Steve Forger and discussed the potential hiccup with Glenn. Steve was pleased that the Governor brought this to his attention, and he assured him that he would get his special branch men on it right away. "Don't respond to him until I get in touch with you, this is exactly why we have assigned the special branch people to you and Catherine, to turn complications into opportunities. If what you suspect is true we may well be able to exploit this to our advantage. If it's bloodletting he's after, we have a few surgeons ourself."

"My accountant did a thorough examination of the books and what Glenn said is true, but there's something unsettling and too convenient in all of this." The Governor expressed.

"Let's see if your nose for machination is as good as you claim, but I agree with you, a junior bookkeeper wouldn't have the imagination for intrigue on this level. There are bigger players behind this. Send the contract over to us along with the ledger of his payments. I'll have our lawyers and accountant have a look as well. The thing that peaks my interest is the paltry amount of money we're talking here. In the scheme of financial fraud, this is relativity a trivial matter." Steve said thoughtfully.

"I would agree, but it's Glenn's character that I don't trust. When he was fired he went without remorse, contrition is not in his nature, nor does he suffer from a moral conscience. His remorsefulness was too Shakespearian for me. As for Jackson, my incumbent, his strategy up to now has been to use his heroic wartime record, being a black African American and jobs, but this looks like a new tactic, and why so late in the running? It can only suggest Jackson's desperate and doesn't think he can win without getting me off message. We're both going on a whistlestop tour in a few weeks so this could be in preparation for that."

"Well, if Jackson is up to dirty politics, we have our own muckrakers as well. Let's hope this works in our favour, and if our guys find something else out in this investigation, all the more ammunition."

They clinked their martini glasses together to acknowledge the plan and separated company.

"Your secretary sent over your campaign schedule, very ambitious. Your starting your whistlestop tour next week, your meeting with the union leaders, you're on 12 campuses, at 18 different factories and business, a number of rallies, sports events, charities and your wife is speaking at numerous women's functions and organizations. I also see you have a hefty rubber chicken circuit as well. Again, as I said before, we are prepared to throw our weight behind you not only with our political support, but with our financial aid as well. And we're going to begin tonight in the area of your TV, radio, billboards and newspaper spots. I've assembled our media team along with some pundits in the Orange room and thought we could get started on a framework strategy and you can help them understand your campaign message better. It's only six months till the election so we want to make this count." Steve said warmly. "I would also like to send you Ted Wilson our campaign manager who you met the night at the hotel in Danton, would you be open to his consultancy?"

"I'm here to win Steve, and like you said, were a team now." the Governor said as he put his hand on Steve's back as a gesture of friendship.

Catherine was spying out the land. Making note of the elegant and the polite, the opulent and the influencers, the dignified and the distinguished. She had already danced with the suave son of a senator and the grandson of a famous civil rights activist. She was grateful there were men under 60 at the event and enjoyed hearing what was in vogue in Washington. That is until Joshua T Potter cut in on one of the dances.

"Hi, I'm a friend of your father and I'm helping him with his campaign, one of his speech writers." Joshua said optimistically, like he was a salesmen at your door. Catherine could see that he definitely was a sanguine personality, good-humored and buoyant in spirit. Her dad was bombastic and authoritative and she could see how Joshua would be good for him.

"How convenient, you must be part of the Washington team, because I know most of his staff and campaign employees?" Catherine remarked.

"Yes, I'm new, I'm currently the Presidents speech writer, but I've been allotted some time to help your father win this senatorial race." Joshua continued.

"The party is bringing out the bigwigs I see, you must have plans for him if you're helping him now?" Catherine said fishing for information.

"The Democratic Party has been taking a beating in the last few elections and were throwing our weight behind candidates who we believe have what it takes to restore and reinvigorate our image and policies once again." Joshua answered with poise and conviction.

"And are you dancing with me because you want to ask me something." Catherine remarked.

"Absolutely, I enjoy working with astute people, it saves all that velvety flattery one has to come up with to look the part. I appreciate straight up honesty, how refreshing in this setting. I can see your a lot like your father in that regard." Joshua said smiling

"Thank you, I take that as a compliment." Catherine said proudly.

"I believe you can have a very positive effect on your fathers campaign. Your demographic are increasing their voting record and it could give your dad the swing vote he needs. Your age group is more than a mircotargeting strategy now, it is a force to be reckoned with. I'm *keen to do a spread on you in the Danton Globe Magazine. With pictures of you engaged in campus life, your role in the entrepreneurs leadership club, your home life and your views on various issues like Rock and Roll, fashion, and women in leadership, giving the people in your state a chance to look inside the life of your father's family. It's the personal, yet endearing touch I believe he needs to win the younger generation. Real issues with the celebrity slant. It's the dream of many kids your age. Would you agree?" Joshua commented enthusiastically.

"I'll suggest getting this article onto the college campuses magazines, or you could do an insert in the newspapers as well. Catherine suggested.

"Brilliant," responded Joshua, "would tomorrow be suitable for you to do the interview and I would like to do a photo shoot of you and your family in Washington D.C.?" Joshua asked expectantly.

"It's fine with me, but I would check with my dad, he's the decision-maker around here." Catherine explained.

"Thanks, and by the way, your looking *chrome plated tonight ." Joshua pointed out.

Catherine responded, "so, you speak our language."

Joshua smiled and said, "I go to Drive-In's, I have to keep up with the latest pop culture so as to keep in touch with your generation."

Catherine turned around to see her dad disappearing into a room with several other men and women. "Catherine, how is the evening going for you?" Her mom asked as she put her arm under Catherine's arm from behind.

"Enchanting mom, dad has conducted himself with dignity so far, you're looking regal and the men have been quite chivalrous. This evening has had the right propriety, protocol and beguiling illusion." Catherine expressed.

"Well, most of my conversations have been with very loquacious women, all talk and no substance. But one trivial remark did perk my interest, it was Mrs. Emerson, she's the wife of the New York senator and they know senator Jackson very well. Our opposition. She didn't know that I was right behind her when she mentioned this because she thought I had left the conversation. It's a trick I learned from your dad. It's what they say when you leave a conversation that is more important than what they say when your talking with them."

"Mom," interrupting her mother, "so cloak and dagger, I've not seen this covert side of you before."

"Politicians wives are connoisseurs of spurious behaviour darling. Watch and learn Catherine, watch and learn. Anyway, she made this off handed remark that Jackson has just developed a new campaign strategy that would assure him his incumbency. She used the words, he's a shoe-in." Her mom repeated.

"Looks like we have something to talk about on the way home tonight." Catherine asserted.

"That's if your father ever gets out of that meeting he just went into." Mrs. Stone said.

It was another hour and a half before the Governor was released from the Orange room. They all emerged with smiles, handshaking and nodding of heads, the gestures that they were all on *cloud nine .

In the limousine on the way back to our hotel mom told dad the interesting tidbit she overheard from Mrs. Emerson. "Yes, I'm well aware of this, as a matter of fact, you remember the bookkeeper Glenn who worked for me when I was Mayor?" "Yes," mom injected, "he was a mousey type of young man. I must say, I never did trust him. In my imagination he always looked like a villain in one of Charles Dickens books."

"Well, he showed up in my office the other day out of the blue claiming he had some vital information that would help me win the election. But Frank and I don't trust him so this Washington team is going to help us sleuth out the truth of it all. But thanks for that nugget of gossip, I can always count on you hon." Her dad replied.

"We're leaving tomorrow at 6pm which means we have to be in Washington Dulles airpot around 4:30, so we'll leave the hotel at 3:00. Traffic is horrendous here in D.C. I have a few meetings to attend at our hotel but you ladies are free to do a little sightseeing if you would like. You haven't been here before Catherine and the sights might inspire you, like the statue of Lincoln, the Capital, or even the White House. I could arrange a special tour for you if you would like. But remember, be back in our room by 2:00 all packed and ready to go.

"We'll come up with something dad, don't worry about us, right mom?" Catherine spoke up. "Absolutely, I'm practically a tour guide myself." Her mom suggested

# CHAPTER 8

# THE CON ARTIST IS REVEALED

*"Don't walk around with a chip on your shoulder, always spoiling for a fight."*

Proverbs. 4:30 MB

Jim and Andy, the two special branch men assigned to Governor Stan entered Glenn's apartment carrying two duffel bags filled with surveillance equipment. They arrived in front of his address in a white van with the sign that said, "Exterminating Done Right." They wore white jumpsuits, white *lids and black shades*. Jim quickly picked the lock on the door and they shouted, "hello, we're here to take care of your pest problem."

His apartment looked like a loner lived there, sparse, lacking in color and imagination. He did however like his toys, Color *Box , Hi Fi system and video games . It all fit his personality, materialistic and self absorbed. Several things were broken in the apartment which showed a lack of self respect. Obviously he never had anyone over. His video game chair was in the middle of the living room with only a few straight back chairs for unexpected guests. His posters were moody, Batman, Attack of the 50 foot Woman, Hot Rod Gang and Dragstrip Riot. . In his bedroom he had a collection of comic books as well. Many of them still in their original wrapping. Unquestionably a man with an over inflatable ego who'd been impeded by the hand life had dealt him. He possessed the bottom end of the gene pool and resented the limitations so cruelly imposed on him, so he escaped into the world of fantasy. Sitting in his video chair he was the conquering hero and there was nobody to tell him otherwise. Andy felt for him. He had investigated these types before and they always ended up in prison or suicidal. They were chronically depressed, lonely and angry. If Glenn was working for someone they knew his type as well and were no doubt manipulating him for their own means. These types of loners were easy prey for people with control issues. Andy had seen how these kinds of people were exploited through emotional blackmail. Pretend your their friend, win their confidence and then they'll do anything for you.

They started putting the listening bugs and miniature cameras around the apartment. In the lamps, the ceiling fan in the bedroom, in clocks, under tables, chairs, and other decor items in the rooms. They continued to put tracking devices in his shoes, pants and jackets . Glenn's life was about to be turned upside down.

"If this guy is a scam artist, we'll know about it pretty soon." Andy said

The Stone's were home from the Washington D.C. trip and Catherine was back at collage. Only a few weeks to go and she would be out. When she came out of her biology class with Hanna she noticed the Chrysler again parked at the end of the school parking lot. "Hanna, there's the car again." Catherine said with concern. "This is really bugging* me."

"You're right, it doesn't look like you're paranoid after all." Hanna remarked.

"We have got to find out who that is, did you find out anything at the library about her or the car?" Catherine asked.

"Nothing, I tried all my tricks but came up empty. I even asked my dad if one of his research guys at work would try to find her and the car and they came up empty as well." Hanna said frustrated.

I'll give it a couple more days, and if that woman still thinks she can be an intrusion into my private life, we'll take matters into our own hands." Catherine said with determination. Oh, and by the way, the 'running' we'd been doing most mornings, I think I'm going to take a break for a while. I've been feeling sick in the mornings. I think I've been pushing myself too much, that OK with you?" She asked

"Sure, I think I'm fit enough for my summer bikini. I've got to run Cath, give you a bell* when I'm free." Hanna mentioned as she started for her *Chariot.

A few days later Andy called Washington D.C. "Sir, this is Andy, Jim and I are looking into the scandal regarding the Governor and his bookkeeper."

"Right, sorry, I was distracted by the pandemonium here at the office today. You'd think we were being invaded or something." Ben replied defensively. Ben was Steven Forgers assistant, the Chairman of the Democratic Party.

"I have the information you requested." Andy shouted above all the noise.

"Great, that was quick, and is it what we hoped for?" Ted asked eagerly.

"Better than we expected, sir, I've sent you a complete detailed summary of all our findings along with all the necessary attachments to verify. I just wanted to alert you by phone to check your special projects mail ." Andy asserted. "He's documenting every single conversation; phone, memo's and carbon copies of money deposits . I think he was saving them to blackmail Senator Jackson if he got into trouble or wanted a payout. We think he was working both sides of the fence."

"We'll have a look at it this afternoon and get back to you if any follow up needs to be done." Ben answered.

"Thanks. Talk to you later." Andy ended the conversation.

"Any further instruction?" Jim asked.

"No, we're to wait until they have had a chance to look over the information, but I can just see their faces when they discover that Glenn was getting paid by Jackson even when he was the bookkeeper for the Governor years ago. The plot is thickening." Andy voiced with a smile.

That afternoon Steven, Alec the party's lawyer, and the chief accountant, Steven's secretary and a few other aides met in Steven's conference room in Washington D.C. to review all the surveillance information, the books and the GreenEver contract with the City of Danton. It wasn't long before they were all smiling.

The lawyer started, "this contract is a fine piece of work. This Senator Jackson must have some astute people working with him. First, the real pearl doesn't even show up until page 172, and then it's in an addendum with very fine print under section miscellaneous. In this section it gives the GreenEver Corporation the right to raise the cost of services every month due to environment condition, inflation and cost of services. I wish I had written a contract like this. They have virally given themselves carte blanche. It's genius. No wonder the person who approved this didn't see this." Alec remarked.

The accountant went next. "From what I can see, the allegations that the charges did escalate are true. But like the contract, there were footnotes made in the back of the accountant ledger, which is an usual way of notating things they want to hide. For instance, why GeenEver continued to charge during the strike. Again, in fine handwritten print, it says, 'garbage continued to be collected outside the strike zone to assist other regions with their demands as well.' So even though they stopped collecting in their contractual region, they continued to operate in other regions. And there's another note here you will be interested in, 'cost escalated due to the amount of garbage collected because of the strike.' So even in the bookkeeping notes they have covered themselves."

Then Alec spoke up, "Listen to this. According to data taken from Glenn's books , he has been receiving supplementary funds from the GreenEver corporation for the past 8 years. He also owns a condo in Orlando and has a substantial retirement fund. It looks like our guy has been at this game for a lot longer than we or the Governor first thought. Along with his data we have photo's of Glenn meeting with Senator Jackson on several occasions. Plus recorded phone calls and memo's . We have more than enough to link these two together."

"So, we have some real backdoor wheeler dealer scheme that has been in the planning for at least 8 years. He's going for entrapment by presenting the truth as fraud. Inventive! This Jackson is no amateur to politics. He has nurtured this subterfuge for a long time and believes this is the hour to dangle the bait to our Governor. He wants the Governor to accuse him of fraud so Jackson can prove that he is in the right, making the Governor look like he lacks integrity, that he is resorting to a smear campaign, and is a poor judge of character. Very astute. Yes, it's the small things that often trip us up. I'll bet you the Governor will be *frosted when he hears this. He'll be so nonplussed he didn't see this earlier that he'll realize he needs us all the more. This is good ladies and gentlemen. We'll, I think the best way to abrogate this potential crisis and prevent the Governor from crossing the Rubicon is to advise him to do absolutely nothing, to not take the bait and let this die a death before it even lives."

Andy received a detailed report from the findings of the committee along with the advice to the Governor in his encrypted file on his desk . The assignment was now to keep an eye on Glenn to see if any further developments emerged with Jackson and meet with the Governor to give him the findings.

That evening at the Governor's residence you could hear Stan shouting vulgarities throughout the house, "that salacious, low-minded, uncouth, ill-bred rat, I'll cook him alive! He's just *cruising for a bruisin."

"I don't believe we should go the self righteousness route, anyone in politics is generally not Lily White." Andy clarified.

"Your right off course, it's just my pride that's been wounded. Jackson has out maneuvered me which is humiliating." The Governor conveyed.

"We also need to be careful, Governor, the strategy here is to do nothing, not get side tracked in this election. We want to remove any edge he was planning. That in and of itself will be infuriating, and could throw him off guard. All the speeches he has already written, all the media spots he has planned will all be for nothing. But there is just one more thing, we think

Glenn made a recording of your meeting with you and Frank, is there anything we should be worried about? Is it necessary for us to retrieve it?" Andy asked firmly

"No, that snake. No, we were very careful not to incriminate ourselves." The Governor said thoughtfully.

"You're sure Governor, is there anything acrimonious that could be taken out of context, then played over radio or TV that could be misconstrued as referring to something else?" Andy reiterated. "Please think carefully, this is not the hour to end up in political quagmire."

"No, we were on to him as soon as we saw him in my office. All we told him was that we would follow up with the acquisitions, and Frank did not promise him anything in return for his information." The Governor assured Andy.

"Like a spider they sat around weaving their plots waiting for me to get caught in their web. Please tell our friends in Washington how appreciative I am of their diligence. If not for them I may have stepped right into their snare." The Governor reflected.

"It was a meticulous plan, but you know as well as I do that the higher up the ladder you go the more powerful and cunning your enemies are. That's why we need each other, sir." Andy stated.

"You can say that again, I'll be calling Steven as well and personally thanking him for all this effort." The Governor said.

Andy left and felt good that he and Jim were seen as valuable to the Governor, it makes his job so much easier when the people he's protecting cooperate and trust him. He was also pleased that Glenn would escape this round of political intrigue to fight his battles another day. Andy knew he was merely a pawn in the machinery and this time he avoided being ground down by the cogs of fate. He could see him now, shouting victory in his living room, surrounded by his best friends Batman and the Gang as he wins another video game. .' He was a stray dog being led astray by acts of misguided sympathy.

CHAPTER 9

# THE UNEXPECTED INTRUDER

*"Why did I reject a disciplined life? Why didn't I listen to my mentors, or take my teachers seriously? My life is ruined!"*

*Proverbs. 5:12-14 MB*

The first year of university was over and everybody dispersed to the four corners of the earth. Nick was in Switzerland with his family on an all inclusive package holiday. They sailed the RMS Empress of Britain from New York to Liverpool, England. Took a train from Liverpool to Dover, a ferry from Dover to Calais, France; and than the train to Basal, Switzerland. His parents sure had the bread*. Jesse was able to spend a week with outbound, biking in Quebec, Canada. Beth and Ann went to Los Angeles for a filmmaking seminar sponsored by MGM and Nicole went to Paris with three other girls. They flew on the new Trans Atlantic passenger jetliner from New York to London on the new British Comet Jet. Hanna was also touring Europe with her parents who bought high end antiques for their business. She was also studying French while she was there as well. Catherine's dad was in full flight with the campaign and wasn't around much now. Catherine had to stay near home because she was helping with the campaign by attending various functions, making speeches, doing interviews, involved in photo ops with Monet and entertaining key young entrepreneurs and leaders. It was all go and Catherine loved it. It was heady stuff.

Everybody would be home in a few days to start their summer jobs at cafe's, sports and department stores, as well as gas stations . Beth and Ann were planning on making their first short film over the summer and submit it to some film festivals. They had already raised $10,000,written a script, and had a friend of theirs who was going to do the music score. They were

60

hoping they would make some valuable contacts in the film industry while in California. Jesse worked every year at "Speciality Cycling" and loved exchanging stories with all the cyclists who came in to have their bikes repaired. Nick didn't have to work so he volunteered as a counselor at the church camp every summer. Organizing sports, leading nature walks, trying to keep the kids quiet at night and generally acting like a child all summer. Nicole loved volunteering at the children's hospital for kids with special needs. She felt needed, loved. It was a real boost to her self esteem.

Catherine was incredibly busy with her obligations to her dad's election. But she also knew that going from a Governor to a Senator had some new perks as well. The short term sacrifice was worth the long term gain. However, her nausea was getting worse and more regular. She made a comment to her mom from the top of the stairs and her reply was, "you're not pregnant, are you?"

"Mom, don't be ridiculous, that's not even funny." Catherine shot back.

"You have been working hard and not getting much sleep, maybe that has something to do with it?" Her mom suggested. "But you might want to go see the family doctor, can't afford you out of commission now."

"Maybe, I don't feel sick now and it only lasts for a short time, I'm sure it will pass." Catherine replied as she walked back into her bedroom. But the comment her mother made about being pregnant scared her, and she thought back to that night with Ted eight weeks ago at Hanna's house.

Catherine drove into Hartford, two towns over from her city and found a corner drug store. A place she thought nobody would recognize her. As she was looking around the store the front door opened with the usual bell and in walked Jesse. Catherine looked instinctively out of guilt and recognized him from their high school. "What's he doing here?" Catherine said with exasperation. She kept her head down and stayed in the back of the store hoping to avoid him.

"Hi Catherine," Jesse called out, "this is an odd place to meet."

"I'm sorry, do we know each other?" Catherine said hoping to deflect attention.

"My apologizes, Catherine, we were in high school together and even had some of the same classes, though none of the same friends, and you came to church with me about 5 years ago, if you remember?" Jesse said self-consciously. He still had his helmet on and was so mesmerized by seeing Catherine that he forgot how dorky he looked in it.

"Jesse, that's right, I think it's the helmet that threw me off, and the fact that you're considerably taller than when I remembered you." Catherine responded while thinking, *and considerably *dreamy as well.* "What brings you to this out of the way establishment?"

"Oh, my Gran just lives a few buildings from here and I often come here to pick up a few essentials for her. She's 89 and doesn't get out much anymore." Jesse said a little uncomfortable as he was holding a tube of hemorrhoid gel in one hand and a stool softener in the other. He was looking down at the items as he was thinking about them and when he looked up she was staring at the two items herself. "These are for her, Jesse said."

"I certainly hope so with someone so fit as you. Otherwise you best get a job in a convalescent home." Catherine said lightheartedly as they both chuckled.

"Well, my Gran needs me so I'll better *split , nice seeing you Catherine." Jesse said with kindness in his voice. "Yeah, you too." Catherine agreed.

When he left she looked around in hope to find some from of pregnancy test. She hadn't heard of any but was hoping to do this discreetly. But there was nothing so she bought some other items to cover up why she came there . As the clerk was ringing up the item, she looked at Catherine and smiled. Catherine blurted out, "Oh, they're not for me, it's my mother." She suddenly realised that she to had bought the same items that Jesse had "My mother is panicking because she's about to take a long trip." The clerk just continued to smile as she gave Catherine the total.

"That was embarrassing, just further proof that kids ruin your life before they're even born. First the nausea, then getting fat, followed by humiliating and uncomfortable doctor examinations, summed up with excruciating labor, and that's just for starters. They're a pain when they come into the world, a heartache when they're in your home and trauma when they leave. Listen to me, I'm talking to myself already, I'm turning into my mom." Catherine then remembered her mom crying in her bedroom because of how disrespectful she was towards her. *I was such a brat, wasn't I?* A melancholy came over her. It was a Daisy Buchanan moment, the rich, beautiful girl of Jay Gatsby's dreams who became his nightmare. Catherine's once enthusiastic life-force would transmute into regret that would cause her to become a shadowy figure if she was knocked up? Could she be pregnant?

When she sat in the drivers seat and put the package on the back seat she erupted with rage, pounding the steering wheel with her fist, stomping her feet on the floor of her car and screaming , "you stupid girl, how could you!" After a minute of pummeling the car she cried tears of despair. When she looked up, she was startled by the clerk who was standing next to her window. She had her hand on her mouth and was crying along with her. Catherine lowered the window and choked out the words, "can I help you?" More out of annoyance than real concern.

"I heard you screaming, and then crying and became concerned. I thought maybe you were feeling alone or scared, but I want you to know, I'll pray for you." This stranger offered.

"I think you have the wrong idea, as I said, they're for my mother, and I don't need you prayers. You're being sweet but this is none of your business, so please excuse me." Catherine spoke with irritation. She raised the window and was cross with herself for *flipping her lid like that. That's exactly what she didn't want - attention. *And by the way, I don't even know if I am pregnant yet, this little escapade may all be for nothing, even though it does seem I'm far more hormonal and touchy.* As she began to see the symptoms mounting her fears were growing.

On the way home Catherine stopped at their family doctor, walked in and asked to see their doctor, saying it was an emergency. The nurse knew Catherine and the family well so she went into the doctors examination room and asked if he could see Catherine Stone as she was saying it was an emergency. "Sure, always happy to see her, just wait until I'm finished with my patient here." Doctor Eugene said.

The other patient came out and Catherine was called in. "Hi Catherine, I understand you have an emergency, how can I help?" The doc say.

Catherine started, "I have a very delicate question to ask you and I first want to know if you could keep my visit private for a little while. My dad in in the middle of his campaign and this could be a major distraction for him, is that possible?"

"I'll do my best to be discreet Catherine, within the law that is." The doc said looking suspicious.

"Thanks, and this may be a shock to you and I know it could be a shock to me if my suspicions are confirmed. I have been feeling nausea in the mornings, and my breasts are a little sore, so I'm thinking that it maybe possible I could be pregnant?

The doctor looked at her like a father, "so, let me ask the million dollar question, did you have sex?"

Catherine put her head down and barely got the words out, "yes, about two months ago.

"Well that will do it, Catherine, and especially at your age, your as fertile as can be right now.So why don't you go into the bathroom and give me a urine sample, I'll have to sent it of to the lab for the results and should have it back in about a week. Than we will know for sure. Have you missed your period as well?" The doctor asked further.

"Yes, so you can see how worried I am, I feel like it's the end of my life, I could choke myself for being so stupid."

Let's wait for the results before we going ending our life just yet, give me a bell* in a week and I let you know over the phone, and then you should

64

come in for an examination and some medical recommendation for caring for yourself and the baby, but until than, drink a lot of water, get to bed early and keep exercising.

A week later and she made the call to the doctor, who told her she was definite pregnant, and they made an appointment for an examination and consultation. She asked the doctor to keep it to himself and that she would tell her father and mother herself. He agreed but said not to take to long because he had an obligation to the whole family as well as to the state board.

*This is so bad, this cannot be happening to me. I was Valedictorian, I'm the Governor's daughter, I want to enjoy college. I'm going to the Elvis concert in six months... I have a life... I'm dead!* She paced around her room having a *hissy fit, swearing. " I'm going to murder Ted! That stupid pig jock!"

Panic-stricken, Catherine collapsed in a pathetic position onto her bed. *My life is over. I wasn't even planning on having kids, ever. This is not happening. Everybody knows my dad and he knows everybody in this State and America. If I have an abortion it will soon be in all the papers. It will ruin him. My parents will kill me! Oh, and Ted's mom, she's the Hospital Administrator at Saint Mary's. This is like a Greek tragedy with no up side to it. Only Ted is no god and I'm certainly not committing suicide. I can't die now. All my relatives are coming to my American Leaders event to hear my speech as part of my dad's campaign.* She thought bitterly of one of the lines from her speech: *The future is pregnant with possibilities.*

She buried her face in her pillow and cried. And cried, and cried. After a long while, she got up and looked at herself in the mirror, she slapped her face as hard as she could making her right cheek crimson red. She sobbed helplessly, crying in such a way that she had not cried since she was a little girl. Real life had entered her bubbled world. She thought about what her main concerns were just yesterday: what shade of lipstick goes with this outfit? Who was she going to go out with? Which shoes best matches my personality? She shook her head, disgusted with how trivial those decisions now seemed. Daddy's little girl was suddenly fading.

The next day Catherine looked into the mirror, a completely different girl, and said , "I can do this. I'm smart, I can come up with something." She put on her formidable face and thought, I'm not going to live my life in the margins. If Grace Kelley can change her destiny then so can I. Catherine could be stubborn, criminally so. But in situations like this, this is where stubbornness paid dividends.

As she drove to Danton Park the thought of facing her friends scared her slightly, but she was determined to be a strong, empowered woman, dependent on no one but herself. Yet despite her best effort she found herself sitting in her car, shouting , "Please God, is this some kind of *royal shaft!" She paused, "what am I doing, praying? What I need is a secret abortion."

She couldn't get her mind off of her situation as she walked through park, thinking how she was going to tell her friends later. When lunchtime came, she went to the 'Tale of Gloucester' cafe, she needed a Root beer float to camouflage her misery. But who was there, narcissistic Ted with his new drop dead* chick*. He glanced at Catherine with a smirk while the girl had a simper on her face. Catherine glared at Ted from time to time, and with every look her anger boiled up, but it was soon followed by an overwhelming sense of helplessness. She couldn't stay, Ted's face was like a horror movie being played over and over. She thought a little retail therapy might help her get her mind off of her pregnancy and spark some possibility thinking.

That evening she was sitting around a table of democratic loyalist with her mother next to her. Her dad was giving a speech on the issues' of crime and corruption, and how his policy of tougher sentencing, faster trials and using community based programs that have a proven history as partners in the criminals rehabilitation could cut the crime rate by 20 percent over the next four years.

Catherine remained quiet the entire time which was totally out of character for her. She normally loved a talkfest, the quid pro quo when crossing swords in conversation. Her dad had drilled her with power words everyday of her life to predispose her for a place in society. But today everybody seemed to be a stranger. She couldn't relate to the superficial gossip and the usual repartee to prove ones upsmanship. Catherine bowed out of the conversation with only the occasional inane comment letting everybody think she was simply being modest.

# CHAPTER 10

# THE PLAN

*"Mortals make elaborate plans, but GOD has the last word."*

*Proverbs. 16:3 MB*

Catherine couldn't face the campaign staff today, her bed seemed to be the only appropriate place for her. Snuggled up in her blanket, the lights out and the shades drawn was her comfort from the bleak future she was facing. Her cunning manipulative mind was numb with blackness. This tour de force of hopelessness was eclipsing all happiness. There was no light at the end of the tunnel, no silver lining or happy ever afters. All she could picture was her dad shouting and screaming, her mom crying, her friends unfriending and the scandal making national headline news. She felt such a scallywag*.

She turned on her transistor radio hoping some new sound* would clam her mind and distract her from her misery. The song, "It's all in the Game", by Tommy Edwards came on with him sing, "Many a tears have to fall, but it's all in the game." She turned the radio off and screamed into her pillow.

But late in the afternoon she found herself at her friends' usual hang out, Hannah's house. Everybody was back from holidays with tans, tales of their adventures and gifts. Hannah's parents remained in Europe to finish their buying but Hannah wanted to be home, so it was free drinks with very comfortable couches. As isolated as Catherine felt, she needed to talk to somebody.

"Hay, Cat, how's the campaign going?" Hannah asked. "I've been following your dad on the news since back Europe and it's looking good, yea?"

"Exceptionally actually," Catherine responded. "It looks like my dad is going to be the next Senator of this State."

"*Nifty" they all said in unison. Ann lifted her mug and proclaimed, "A toast to our very own Senator's daughter, to knowing the rich and famous, and having access to new persuasive powers in high places when we get ourselves in a tight spot." As they drank Catherine fell into her chair expressing, "I'm exhausted." Which was just enough to change the topic and take her out of the center of their *chinwag .

Her usual close friends were there, Hannah, Beth, Nicole, Ann and to her surprise Ted and his girlfriend were there. They were in the back garden having a look around the property because they had never been there before. When they walked in Catherine got the shock of her life. He never came to Hannah's house. What was he doing there? Come to find out, Ted's girlfriend was Ann's cousin and she invited them.

Ted was nervous when he saw Catherine and made some lame excuse about having to attend summer football practice, and needed to split*. He was a horrible liar and everybody could see that he just wanted to *split from there but nobody knew why. Ted knew he had taken advantage of Catherine at the party but wasn't sure if she remembered much of anything. His girlfriend looked uneasy and embarrassed because of the quick exit, but Catherine was relieved to say the least.

Hannah was making another round of drinks and was looking more Parisian than ever while Nicole was setting the table with more chocolate croissants, and an assortment of pastries. Hannah knew how to do it right, she had Lipton tea, coffee with cubed brown sugar, 7 up, Orange Crush, and RC cola, Vanilla shakes with cherries on top and Coke A Cola. . She had traveled to Europe every summer with her parents on their business trips because it was the place to find the exquisite rare pieces. Her two favorite places were Paris and Florence. We all envied her but she was never made us feel underprivileged. Not that we were, but Paris, it's every girls dream.

The girls were all on *cloud nine with their news and rest of summer plans while Catherine remained quiet. She broke into the conversation when she finally managed to get up the courage to speak. "I have an announcement." They all stopped speaking a bit alarmed by her behavior and interruption. Then they starred at her with curiosity written on their faces.

"What I have to tell you is a monumental secret, and, if any of you tell anybody, I swear I will tell my father about you taking your parents drugs and the police will never leave you alone. Understand?" They all nodded, some more hesitant than others. "I know we're good friends and most of the time I conduct myself with decorum and am fairly good-natured, but you also know that you don't want to be on my bad side. I'm sorry I'm acting so mean but what I'm about to share with you is Kryptonite."

"You all with me? They nodded and moved in closer to make a huddle. "All right, " Catherine said. "You've seen the movie, the Man Who Knew to Much."

"Yeah, yeah ".They all said.

"Well, that's how serious I am about this secret, and I'll know if any of you say a word." Catherine said. "You know the party we went to two months ago at Hannah's...." She stopped. All eyes were on her.

"Yeah," Hannah said.

Catherine decided to forego the details. She skipped straight to it, "The unthinkable has happened. I'm knocked up*." She tried to make her tone sound serious and light, but instead she came off awkward, and it hung dryly in the air. There was a short, stunned silence before a hysterical chorus of voices pumping out questions like a fire hydrant at her:

"What?"

"Are you serious?"

"Catherine!"

"*On the hook*."

"No, I'm not on the hook, but the pregnancy is real. , Catherine said

"Whose baby is it?"

"What are you going to do?"

"So, whose baby is it?"

"Does your dad know?"

"That will *rattle your cage!"

Catherine was overwhelmed by all the comments flying at her from all directions. She put her head down and silence filled the room. Everyone was stunned and shocked. Their idol had fallen. The perfect Valedictorian, the Governor's daughter, the homecoming queen, the most popular and desired girl in school, was smeared. At the vision of Catherine becoming fat, pregnant and wadding, their faces became dismayed.

Hannah lamented how tragic it was that it had happened at her party. She started thinking back to who it could be but everybody was so *loaded that the night that is all became a blur. "Cat," she said, "if I hadn't thrown that party, you wouldn't be in this mess."

*Why does she have to turn this situation into her deal?* Thought Catherine, but she only said, "Don't worry, Hannah. If it hadn't happened at your place, it would have only happened somewhere else. Trust me. I was in the mood that night!" She was trying to joke around and remain being their *cool, sophisticated leader, but she could see her time as queen bee was quickly descending.

Catherine looked at her watch and interrupting everyone's chatter she stood up to walk out, she asked them to come over to her house later to further clue them in on her ordeal . She had, by now, thrown out her previous philosophy of, "doing it herself," and figured that together they could come up with some sort of plan.

"Sure, we're with you, Cat!" They all said.

Catherine walked out of Hannah's house and before she got into her car Catherine noticed the black Chrysler again parked about a half a block away. She thought, *It's definitely following me. This is not good. What are they after, what do they want? As if having to deal with this pregnancy was not enough, now I have to come up with a way of flushing her out. And I'm in the mood for some guerrilla tactics, but you later.*

Her friends came over one by one that evening. Her mom was there to greet them with coffee and Hors d'oeuvres. Her mom was the queen of hospitality and had a way of winning people to her side. Oscar Wilde said, "Some cause happiness wherever they go; others whenever they leave." She was the person in the first half of that saying. Catherine was happy that her mom was setting the mood for her 'closing curtain' get together.

Hannah, her best friend, arrived first. Catherine was sophisticated, but Hannah had that cosmopolitan personality, all those European trips and boyfriends in every country gave her an air of cultural finesse. Catherine's mom loved to talk to her because she had gone to Paris on her honeymoon and Hannah was a way to revive the romance her and Catherine's dad once had before politics became his world. She had those unguarded eyes that drew you in to sharing your secrets with her.

Nicole came second; she was anorexic because her home life was abusive. Her dad was an alcoholic and her mom was addicted to prescription drugs. Even her cat was neurotic, or at least bulimic. Poor thing could never keep her food down. But Nicole was exceptionally smart and a research genius.

Beth and Ann came in together, laughing as usual. Beth could quote any movie line and Ann knew the words to almost any song. They were loquacious and once they got on a roll there was no stopping them, you would be laughing so hard it would be difficult to even breathe. They were majoring in film and acting, something they were born for. Together they formed a synchronize vibration.

Once they were all comfortable in Catherine's bedroom she said, "Ok, I need a plan for how I'm going to get out of this. But, whatever we say here doesn't leave the room. Agreed?"

They all looked at each other with that secretive smile and said, *"Neat!"

Catherine took a deep breath and began: I can't tell my parents who really got me pregnant because his parents are big contributors to my dad's campaign, and they're golf partners. This would destroy their relationship and the flow of money into my dad's campaign. And that would mean I would have a very *frosted father."

"I think he'll have a *cow anyway," Nicole said

"No, he'll be happy!" Hannah said. She turned towards Catherine. "Wouldn't he be happy? You marry the son of a big contributor....that would be good, wouldn't it? Like the royal families did in Europe long ago.

"I don't want to *circle this guy," Catherine answered." Besides, he would never admit he did it, anyway. To *circle him would mean my life would be over."

Hannah couldn't restrain herself, she had to know. "You keep talking about, 'this guy,' when are you going to tell us who it is, we're dying here!"

Catherine put her head down and said, "I can't, I'm not ready for that yet."

Beth hugged her. "It's OK; you're the one who's been taken advantage of."

Ann said, "You've worked too hard to give up your perfect life. So, why not get an abortion? I mean, you didn't ask for the baby."

Catherine sighed. "I thought about it, but my Dad's the Governor and knows everybody. The papers could learn about it and he'll be the latest front page scandal. And we have to be even more careful about it because the elections are coming up in November. This kind of press would crush him and my mom."

"We'll fly you out of state…" Hannah said.

Catherine began to cry softly. "It's less than a month to giving my speech at the Leaders event, then there's numerous campaigning events, plus I'm helping my dad reach out to our generation. He wants me to gain some experience in this area. I could never get out of it now. My parents have every moment of my life planned. I don't have time to fly off somewhere, let alone recover from an abortion! Besides, I wouldn't even risk doing it out of state. I mean - My dad's the Governor, and he's running for State Senator!"

"*No sweat," Beth said, having never seen Catherine cry so hard before. "What if you blamed this on someone your parents don't like? Then maybe they'd suggest you get an abortion instead of getting married. And if your dad is behind it he could keep it a secret, he has power and connection."

"Like a teacher!" Ann said. "Just don't name him."

There was a slight pause, and then Catherine's face lit up. "Now were cooking with gas*," Catherine said. Suddenly, energy filled the conversation about who could be this person whose's *nowhere. They decided that a teacher would be too *raunchy to keep out of the papers, so they thought to look in the direction of a student. They went through name after name, person after person, but no consensus came. Catherine felt a little hope that abortion could be in the cards; they just had to figure out who they could blame. Finally, Beth pulled out Catherine's yearbook from High School, thinking that some of these students are in her classes at College. "We are going to go through this book and find you a victim to pin this on," she said.

No one seemed right. There were problems with almost every guy. Some of the boys Catherine genuinely liked as friends and didn't want to hurt them. Others, even her father wouldn't believe she'd sleep with. Some boys, she feared, would take it to court. Then...................

"Wait, who's this?" Hannah said. "He's a dreamboat! Does he go to our college?"

"Yeah," Ann said. "His name's Jesse. I know him from my Bio class in High School."

Catherine glanced at his photo.

"How do I not know this *Dreamboat?" Hannah said. "Why hasn't he been coming to our parties and *necking with me?"

"Well, he's kind of... you know," Ann answered.

"No. What?" Beth said.

"He's a Christian, one of those *squares who's always like 'Jesus this, Jesus that'. So he's not, like, cool or anything. He's never at parties or anything of importance."

"I am definitely going to have to start going to church if that's what they're keeping hidden in the pews," Hannah said.

"Hey, focus," Catherine said, snapping her fingers. "It's my life here!"

"This is your savior," Beth said, making the sign of the cross. "I think he'd work, Cat."

"I actually went to church with Jesse five years ago and even thought Christianity was an option. We were also in classes together in high school, he's a *kookie guy but they don't, like, have sex."

"That's why it would work," Ann said, suddenly excited. "because Christians are always hypocrites, right? And your dad hates Christians, isn't faithlessness his faith? Your dad would definitely be furious. He'd make you get an abortion in a heartbeat." They was silent for a moment, each one mentally associating the word abortion with the word heartbeat, but none of them said anything.

"You could even say he *shafted you on a date. ." Beth added, "Like, all that pent-up sexuality gone mad."

Catherine was quiet. She looked at Jesse's photo, then at her own photo further down the page. In it, she looked so carefree, not a worry in the world. She sighed. "Okay," she said, more to herself than to her friends. "I'll do it. Soon it will be all over. Daddy will *flip his lid , Mom will cry, Daddy will send me off to get the abortion, and he will tell Jesse to *drop dead."

"Yeah," said Beth, "and Jesse's life will be flushed down the toilet!"

"Sounds perfect," Hannah added. "You always do know how to vilify someone."

Nicole, the only one who came from an abusive home piped in, "I know what it's like to be a victim, to take the blame and be mistreated for the faults of others. Your playing a pernicious game here Catherine, you might want to think about this before you flush Jesse's life down the drain."

Nicole was being flooded with memories she had long ago suppressed. She was five again, sitting on the stairs with her mom at the top and her dad at the bottom. He was shouting at her mom with raised fist and her mom was crying while screaming back at her dad. He then ran up the stairs pushing Nicole aside to start smacking her mom. Her mom was than on the floor and her dad grabbed her hair and dragged her down the hall disappearing into their bedroom. Nicole sat terrified in the hallway crying. Than Catherine's voice brought her back to the present.

"I don't have a choice here; it's either me or him, or someone like him. And I can tell you now, if it's a choice between my life being flushed down the drain or someone else's, I will always chose the other persons life to be sacrificed. This plan is like drinking a Root Beer Float, it's so good yet so bad.

I know my dad is home tomorrow from his whistle-stop tour so it's a possibility in the afternoon. "Catherine said. "I'll invite Jesse over to my house, and while he's on his way I'll tell my dad. He will be surprised, Jesse will be clueless and I'll be the victim. Jesse will walk straight into Daddy's fury.... he wouldn't know what to do. I'll call you later with the news!"

Nicole, Ann, Beth, and Hannah sat watching Catherine as she went over the plan again in her mind. "Okay, conspirators," Catherine said. "I think I am going to be just fine. It's all happening tomorrow providing Jesse and my father are available, and remember, you're sworn to secrecy."

Catherine got up from the bed where everyone was sitting and looked out the window. She wanted a moment to reflect on the consequences that could follow the conversation with her dad tomorrow. The four girls were watching in silence as they saw their friend and princess calculate the destruction of an unsuspected victim in order to maintain her selfish lifestyle. This was the real deal, not idle gossip, petty revenge because of a school prank, or smearing someone's reputation. This was the big leagues because it was going to affect Jesse for the rest of his life with devastating repercussions. This was something her dad would do. Now it was something Catherine was doing with calculating cruelty. She was all grown up. The four girls looked at each other and came to a collective *eureka, their education in cool was over, they had now graduated and where transcending their High

76

School adolescent games, they had just added steroids to their former days of pranks. Now they were changing people's fortunes and manipulating lives to suit their future dreams. It was a chilling yet exciting moment. Nicole, however, was sad that she was agreeing with her friends, she didn't think she had such deviousness in her.

Nicole realized how much she needed their approval and acceptance. Her friends had become her surrogate family and she was not prepared to lose them now. But it meant that she was now becoming the abuser, the one thing she had vowed never to be to someone else. It was a Job moment, "the thing she had feared the most had come upon her.1" She had not anticipated this happening. How could she? Her emotions were beginning to cascade over her.

Nicole bravely interjected into the chatter of the girls on the bed, "what about his family, have you considered them? What if they confront your dad, or even fight it, what if Jesse denies it and goes to the police? It wouldn't be long before the papers or some journalist sniffed it out and started reporting it.

Catherine replied, "I know my dad, he'll expend such pressure on the family that if they do chose to go face to face with him they will end up looking guilty whether they are or not. He'll tar and feather them before they even leave the meeting. "

Nicole responded meekly, "It's just a shame, and I know what shame can do to a person. You all have helped me overcome it by being my friends but this is what I've been going through my whole life."

Catherine broke in, "That's exactly the point, we want shame to drive Jesse and his family into obscurity, or even force them to move away from Danton. We want this problem to go away. If we can paint enough scapegoat-graffiti on him than he or his family will not want the public humiliation."

"But that's so cruel Catherine." Nicole said with a quivering voice, she was beginning to empathize with the pain Jesse would go through. "You're going to assassinate his character."

Catherine didn't skip a beat, "I told you I had a bad side, and one of the things that makes us all such good friends is that we're basically vain by nature, so are you with us Nicole? Are you a flat-earth person whose perception is defined by fear, or are you a round earth person who is willing to sail into glory." Catherine could feel her fears dissolving away like snow.

Nicole looked at Catherine and the other three girls who were giving her that acid stare, "You know I'm with you, I'm just trying to help us all think it through..."

"*Swell . It's what we call in the game of politics, a sacrificial lamb." Catherine broke away from the conversation by asking, "Besides Hannah and myself, have any of you seen this Chrysler around before?"

The girls jumped up and all shoved in together around the window looking where Catherine was pointing. There it was, the black Chrysler parked about half a block away, the same distance from Hannah's house when Catherine came out that afternoon.

"Looks like a drug dealer or a playboy's car", said Beth. Catherine answered arcanely, "Hannah and I have seen the driver, she looks like a university student or an athletic model, but seeing it tonight is the fourth time. It's following me for some reason."

"Should we walk over to the car and act like we'd had too much to drink," Ann and Beth said excitedly, "it could make a plot for our movie."

"Doesn't look like a woman's car, too government looking," remarked Nicole. "But I could see myself going for a ride in it."

"That's what struck us odd as well, which is why we waited outside my house to see who the driver was. And she's a well-built *Classy chassis , believe you me." Catherine emphasized.

"Could all of you keep and eye out for it, to see if it's near your houses," Catherine said with concern. "I don't want to sound paranoid but four times in a few days is a little concerning."

"I have to *split ," Beth said, "promise you'll give us a *bell and tell us everything?"

They all left but Hanna, who said, "You were quite mean with Nicole earlier tonight, Cath."

"She was getting too sentimental on us. I know she's had it rough, but this is not about her, it's about me and my future. If Jesse and his parents don't go all *hissy fit on us, it can be handled discreetly and with the minimum of collateral damage. My dad will not want this to go public any more than I do. I'm just trying to nudge dad and this situation in the right direction. My aim is not to discredit Jesse in front of the world, but for him to be our lightning rod that attracts all the attention away from me. Believe me; my dad will want to keep this incident private." Catherine said with annoyance.

"Just remember Cath, she's your friend, and has been since junior high school." Hanna said with disquieted tones.

"I know Hanna, it's just this pregnancy, my emotions are all over the place. And I'll only admit this to you, but I'm finding it difficult to keep my fears ring-fenced. There's an alien-force inside of me that is influencing every thought, every emotion and every decision of my life. I'm being reduced to a host. That's what has me so *flipped out Hanna." Catherine related. Hanna walked over and put her arms around Catherine saying, "we're here to help Cath, and I believe Nicole probably understands you more than anyone, she's is only trying to help."

"I know, I just can't afford any weakness right now, and I need for all of you to be strong for me as well." Catherine said.

"We will, Nicole is faithful and would never desert her friends, you can count on her." Hanna reinforced.

Catherine continued to look out the window at the Chrysler . She couldn't tell if anybody was in it and said out loud, "I think we should walk towards the car and see what happens, if it's just my conspiratorial nature, an unlikely coincidence or my feeling of suspicion than nothing will happen."

They walked outside and slowly sauntered across the road to where the Chrysler was parked, they put on their *lids and meandered down the street looking at the houses and gardens as they went. The Chrysler 's engine started up, pulled out of its parking place, made a u-turn and headed down the street away from Catherine. It was a warm summer night just turning twilight so it was difficult to see anybody in the car, plus the windows were tinted.

Catherine turned around and they were concerned now. Was somebody really following her, did it have something to do with her pregnancy, was she a target for kidnapping because of her father's run for Senator? She was confused and apprehensive as they jogged back home. Then she had a thought, *I wonder if some anxiety would cause the baby to be aborted naturally. It has happened in some cases.* Hanna gave Catherine another hug before driving off as well as assuring her that together they would win.

In the house Catherine thoughts went back to the plan. She had always believed that she was writing her own play for her life, but now it seemed someone else was attempting to alter it for her, and this thought snapped her out of her apprehensiveness and made her angry. She thought, *If my daddy is getting the chance of a lifetime, then I'm not forfeiting mine. The plan is good and daddy will be all the more motivated to make this all go away with the presidency dangling over his future.* Straightaway her guileful confidence returned in full strength. She would just have to stage it right so her dad didn't think she was manipulating him, but convince him that she was the victim in all of this. It was a gambit, but one she had played many times before that always ended with theatrical applause.

Catherine pulled up her dad's campaign schedule to see when the next available date would be when she could tell him, and hoped Jesse was available as well. Tomorrow her dad had a two hour window in the afternoon, *this could work,* she thought, than suddenly Catherine's heart came bursting through her ribs as she thought of telling her daddy about Jesse and the baby. Her fears started painting her a bleak scenario.

Just when she believed there was some hope, her future abruptly evaporated leaving a foreboding premonition of ruin. Her *cage was being rattled. .

- 1 Job 3:25 NKJV

# CHAPTER 11

# THE DILEMMA

*"Souls are saved by truthful witness and betrayed by the spread of lies."*

*Proverbs. 14:25 MB*

Nicole drove home slowly because she knew there was nothing waiting for her but more heartache. She saw the sign for Plymouth Park and decided to take a stroll there. It was early evening and most of the walkers would have gone home by now. The park was named after the early settlers from Britain who came to America to escape religious persecution. There were statues of Thomas Hooker, Roger Williams and John Cotton, a miniature village that gave you a sample of what life was like in the 1600's. There were plaques giving history lessons on the various religious movements, the Puritans, Episcopalians, the Separatists and the Congregationalist. At the entrance of the park were two pillars, one holding a miniature model of the famous ship, the Mayflower, and the other pillar housing a recreation of the Mayflower Compact, an agreement to establish civil government under the sovereignty of King James 1. History was inescapable in Danton, you were reminded of it no matter where you went, the Shops , outside of churches, in government buildings, names of streets and historical buildings.

As Nicole walked through the park she was having to deal with her own history. She was shaken, her feelings being ignited by the conversation she just had with her friends at Catherine's house. That sick cramping she got in her stomach when her old man* became violent from too much drinking or her *old lady screaming curses and slander from her prescription drug addiction, and now she was experiencing the same discomfort. That's why she hated to eat food. Food became physically repulsive when she felt like that.

But this was the first time she ever had cramping because of her friends. She felt like her world was closing in on her. He friends had always been her coping mechanism, her oasis, her safe house. Now who was she going to go to. This is why she was bitterly angry with Catherine. Catherine could have any boy she wanted, but that wasn't enough, now she had to *put down an innocent student as well. And here's Nicole, heartbroken because she thought love would never come knocking at her door. Who wants a broken, anorexic loser? She would do anything to *score a boy like Jesse, even if he was a Christian.

Another memory forced itself to her consciousness. She was 13 this time and was watching her dad and mom cat fighting in the living room. He had her in a headlock with one arm and was slapping her head with his other hand spewing out abuse while mom was clawing his arm with her nails drawing blood. It was when Nicole said she was calling the police that they both stopped and her dad left the house.

*Maybe I should warn Jesse.* thought Nicole. "Catherine has unspeakable pride and will turn on me, but I don't think I could live with myself if I consented to being a part of Jesse's demise. It's too horrible." Nicole mumbled to herself. "Now what was his last name? I think I still have my yearbook at home, I'll get his surname and call information for his number." She ran back to her car holding her stomach because of the intense pain. A gnawing apprehension was growing. Time was of the essence.

When she pulled into her driveway she saw her father's Cadillac and mother's Oldsmobile parked in front of the house. She was surprised because her dad had left for a business trip two days ago and wasn't expected for another three days. As she approached the front door she felt unbearably unhappy. Somehow Catherine's scheme had unearthed a lifetime of mistreatment.

She opened the door and could hear her mother crying, sobbing from the kitchen table. She walked into the hall, through the living room and as she entered the dining room to reach the kitchen, her dad spoke from behind her. He was sitting on the coach in the living room, in the dark.

"Your mother's a sick woman, Nicole." Her dad said sarcastically. "And she's obnoxious, inane, useless and an addict. She should be in rehab. Why do you love her, she's a *closet case!"

"And your a boorish drunk who rattles out his pe..jor....a..tive remarks like a tin pot exc...u..tive whose heart is pickled in alco...hol." Nicole's mom screeched out her slurred words with her fist raised in the air defiantly.

Nicole was frozen in-between the two of them, physically and emotionally. Her father and mother were shouting abuse at each other over her head like two galley ships firing canon balls off their bows. And before she could make a decision on what to do or where to hide, her father announced.

"Your mother and I are getting a divorce. I've been asked to move to Geneva, Switzerland to head up our European branches, and I'm not planning on coming back to this menopausal, loathsome *Mickey Mouse ." The father announced with icy accuracy.

All those years of unrequited hope flooded into Nicole's consciousness and the sense of unfulfilled parental love caused Nicole to snap. The years of violent abuse, neglect, screaming, living with endless fear and anxiety coupled with the apprehension of the day with Catherine came boiling out of her like a Vesuvius. She ran into the kitchen and grabbed a knife from the block of wood on the counter and ran towards her father with flaming ferocity, shrieking, "I hate you, I hate you." The father stood up with his alcoholic eyes wide alert, stunned and bewildered as he watched his daughter in slow motion lunging toward him with the knife raised high in her hand. She was on him before he knew what to do.

Nicole stepped on top of the coffee table that was in front of her dad and leaped up into the air, as she was coming down the father tried to jump backwards behind the coach but as he went up and she came down the knife sank deep into the fathers left thigh and he fell back into the coach with Nicole on top of him pounding him with her fists in a rage. She was hysterically unrestrained, she had *flipped her lid after years of torment. Blow after blow to his face, his chest, his neck and shoulders, indiscriminately hitting with her fingernails scratching his face. The father finally reacted in self-defense and bear hugged her so she was unable to hit any more. But Nicole was in a homicidal craze and started biting his nose and lips and cheeks causing excruciating pain with blood gushing from the father's mouth.

The mother looked on in shock, completely horrified by this family scene . Was this her daughter? The father let go of his bear hug and pushed Nicole off. She flew into the air landing on top of the glass and metal coffee table that shattered into a million pieces. Her body was slumped in the middle of the table with her head and legs hanging over the metal edges. Nicole was unconscious, blood dripping down from her neck and legs.

The father's face looked lacerated and his neck was covered with blood from the bites Nicole gave him. The father stood silent, the mother crying and now kneeling beside her daughter, with both of them thinking the worst. "Is she alive?" the father asked his wife. "I don't know, I don't know, what have you done?" She looked up with tears pouring down her face and choked out, "You monster, you killed your own daughter. You're a murderer, a murderer"....and then she fainted from the emotional shock.

Fear took hold of the father and he abruptly became aware that he had a knife sticking in his leg. He slumped back into the coach, took hold of the knife with both hands and slowly pulled it out of his leg. Blood flowed out dripping from his pants onto the rug below. He pulled his belt off and made a tourniquet to stop the bleeding. He then put his leg up on the broken coffee table to slow the flood of blood as well. His hands were trembling, his heart throbbing, and a sense of foreboding came over him. His demons were tormenting him. A trial, prison, his career ended, his family lost, his whole world gone in a moment of time. He was finding it difficult to breath as the thoughts raced through his mind.

When his wife, Coco, came to, she raised herself up and saw her husband sitting in front of her with the knife in his hand and blood everywhere. Jonathan, the dad was jarred out of his thoughts when he saw Coco getting up, "you OK hon?"

"Since when did you care about me?" Coco said with a shaken voice.

"Let's not fight now, we have a crisis on our hands." The dad said angrily. "We! You mean you have a crisis on your hands, I didn't push her, I'm not the one who beat her all these years and caused her to have a psychotic break like that." The mom replied.

"That's good, that's what I'll tell the police, that she had a psychotic episode and went berserk. After all, she did attack me and I was only defending myself." The dad said with some relief.

"Your sick, you know that, you can say whatever you want, but just remember, I have been here for the past 19 years of your daughters life and I know the whole story, not just what happened here tonight." The wife declared.

Jonathan called 999 and a woman answered, "999 , this is Danton police precinct, what is your emergency."

Jonathan answered, "we've had a domestic disturbance and my daughter is...."

The 999 police woman asked, "Is your daughter hurt?"

"Yes," the dad replied, "you need to send an ambulance as well. She's bleeding from her neck."

"Is your daughter alive sir?" Can you feel a pulse on her wrist or on the side of her neck?"

Jonathan asked his wife to feel the side of Nicole's neck to see if she was alive. Coco reluctantly reached down and put two fingers on the side of her neck. Jonathan shouted, "Press harder."

"Her neck is throbbing, I guess that's her pulse." The mom said.

"Yes, we have a pulse, good heavens," he yelled out to the police woman. "Please stay clam and don't try to move your daughter, the ambulance will be on it's way and will be there shorty. And just stay where you are, don't move about, can you do that for me?" The 999 operator said in a very calming voice. She then continued to ask a series of questions, "What is your current address?" How old is your daughter? Is there anybody else hurt in the house? Jonathan answered the questions in a monotone voice as he stared at his daughter's broken body.

Coco and Jonathan both heard the police car and the ambulance sirens. Coco started crying again and the fear returned to Jonathan. He sat there still in the dark with only the light from the kitchen shinning through illuminating the floor while Coco was kneeling on the floor next to Nicole, his daughter's lifeless looking body draped across their Cattelan Italia Dielle coffee table. Tears welled up in his eyes as he remembered how happy he was when they brought her home from the hospital the day she was born. "We were in love, we were happy... what went wrong?" Jonathan was lost in thought when the police banged on his door shouting, "This is the police, open up sir."

Jonathan's leg was not noticeably painful but his pants were covered in blood so Coco went over and opened the front door. The police men stepped in and shinned their flash light on Coco, she had some blood on her blouse and she looked like she was in shock. "Where are your daughter and husband ma'am?" She just pointed and the two police men moved through the hall and into the living room shinning their lights with their hands on their guns in a semi crouched position. When the light shone on Jonathan and the girl the policeman said, "Can you show me your hands sir?" Jonathan raised his two hands and Coco turned the living room light on. The two policemen walked over to the scene and could see Jonathan's leg bleeding and his face all cut up. It looked like cats had attacked his face. Aaron, the first policemen put his two fingers on the girls' neck artery and felt a strong pulse. The second policemen, Raymond, started taking assessing the crime scene. Aaron

87

called the situation in, "we have a possible 123, 133, 216 or 240. Send the detectives and some back up please." A minute later three ambulance personnel came running through the front door and the policemen moved aside to let them handle the girls' body.

It was difficult work because of all the broken glass and the precarious position of Nicole's body. The three paramedics had to handle Nicole's body with delicacy due to possible life threatening neck and leg injuries. But before they could lie her down they had to remove all the bits of broken glass that were protruding from her backside. They soon had her immobilized on the cot with the IV in her arm, a cardiac monitor hooked up, the oxygen mask around her mouth, blood pressure cuff on her arm, splints around her legs and a spinal collar on her neck so they could roll her out to the ambulance. The mother started to throw herself on Nicole and one of the paramedics had to restrain her as to not cause any more harm. By now two more squad cars had pulled up and there were eight policemen and women in the house now. One of the policewomen took Coco and sat her down in the kitchen .

A second ambulance had arrived and the medical personnel were attending to Jonathan's leg and face. They gave him a shot of morphine to ease the pain so he was in no condition to answer any questions. They put Jonathan into the second ambulance and took him to the hospital as well. In the house the policemen and women were talking amongst themselves while a photographer was taking more pictures and others were gathering what they thought might be evidence, even though they were not able to piece together what actually happened. The policewomen could see that Coco was either in shock or on some medication or drug. She was weeping one minute and dispassionate the next, acting capriciously. When the policewomen did ask her a question, she just stared at her with vacant despondency.

The lead investigator said, "This is what we're going to do. The daughter is unconscious, the husband, if that's who he is, will be treated in the hospital and the wife, if that's who she is, is in no condition to answer questions or give an accurate account of what happened here tonight, so let's finish up with the crime scene. The forensics team and photographer will stay on... and Lake, you stay here and have a look around the other rooms for further evidence. Maria and Jennifer, you take Coco to the hospital for an examination to find out what is going on with her and watch over her. We will question the man at the hospital tomorrow, and the woman, you ladies bring her down to the police station tomorrow if the doctors release her. But I want her staying in overnight, she could be a possible suicide threat from the trauma and the drugs it looks like she's on. If they do feel she's a harm to herself we can have her committed for 72 hours, but if not I'll see you at the station tomorrow. Hopefully the daughter will be conscious or still alive. Arron and Raymond, I'll meet you back at the station after you question the man at the hospital and we'll go over what you know since you were the first on the scene. OK everybody, you happy with that?" They all acknowledged Philip the investigator and soon everyone was gone.

The forensic team stayed on to finish their end of the investigation and Lake, another policewoman, was told to remain at the house until everybody left.

CHAPTER 12

# THE EVIDENCE KEEPS MOUNTING

*"You can't keep your true self hidden forever; before long you'll be exposed."*

*Luke 12:2 MB*

The two policewomen managed to get Coco, Nicole's mom, to the hospital. She became belligerent once she was alone with the policewoman in the car where she poured out a litany of complaints against her husband, making him out to be a draconian dictator. Then when the anger dissipated she degenerated into a sordid pitiful heap, which eventually landed her in a fatal position in the backseat of the squad car.

Lake, the policewoman who was staying at Coco's house went to find something to eat. But passing through the living room with the lights on with the forensic team still working, she could see the blood on the couch, floor and broken coffee table. There were footprints, small pools and smears of blood around the furniture. Lake was a rookie and this was her first real crime scene. She lost her appetite and went into the library to look for any letters or incriminating evidence.

It was going to be a long night and Lake needed something to keep her mind occupied. She looked over at the books, "Ah, Mansfield Park, a Jane Austen book, my favorite author." She put her hand on the top of the binding to pull the book out but as she did she saw a glimmer of light behind it. She pulled it out and pulled several other books out too but the light seemed to disappeared. She moved from side to side to see if she was just seeing things but when she went to the left it shined through the back of the bookshelf just briefly. She wondered if there was a room behind the wall of books. She walked out of the room and went into the adjacent room, which

90

was an office, but there were no lights on. She went back into the library and pulled more books off the shelf. She ran her hand up and down on the inside of the shelves as well as on the top and bottom of the shelves thinking there may be some type of latch or button. Her fingers found a round metal plate which she pressed on and the whole bookshelf popped open. *Wow, a secret room. This family is messed up, and wealthy.* She thought to herself.

She opened the door slowly until it was wide open, she wanted to make sure it didn't spring shut on her once she went in. There were stairs that led down, once in, it looked like a second living room. Couches, chairs, coffee table, end tables and lamps. To the far side was a very long desk with several computers , and everything was on. As she walked toward the computer screens she could tell it was a surveillance system. Much like they had at the police station. The cameras were showing angles from inside and outside of a beautiful house with extensive grounds. The cameras were inside the garage, around the pool and on the front street of the property. There was several men and women eating at the dining room table and she could hear them talking, but it wasn't English. It sounded French or kind of German. Lake looked around the room again and spotted some filing cabinets. "What is going on here, why would this guy or the wife or both be spying on this place?" She said out loud.

The father, Jonathan, had been taken to the hospital with the two policemen, Aaron and Raymond staying with him. While the doctor and nurse were attending to his lacerations he was spewing incendiary remarks in a steady stream of consciousness to the two policemen. The doctor asked him to stop talking as it made his job impossible. He gave Jonathan a local anesthetic so he could devitalize pieces of skin and excise the subcutaneous tissue. The nurse followed up with cleaning and suturing the wounds.

The morphine was wearing off and Jonathan's defensive mechanisms were kicking in. He was deflecting the whole incident and accepting no responsibility for Nicole's condition. Jonathan was naturally a high adrenaline personality and the police were getting frustrated with his uncooperative attitude. It was clear to them that there was no remorse or sadness about the condition of his daughter, as a matter of fact, he never once inquired about her. He just kept justifying his own actions. Jonathan started up again, "You know she never said a word during the whole assault, what was she thinking, why did she freak out like that?"

"We don't know sir, but that's what we're attempting to piece together." Aaron answered him. "What do you think lead your daughter to attack you so viciously?" Inquired Raymond.

"I suppose it's the fact that her mom and I are getting a divorce. Coco and I were having one of our many disagreements when she walked in and heard us arguing." Jonathan said flatly.

"Did she become part of the argument?" Raymond asked further.

"No, she never said a word, she just stood there, mute." Jonathan related.

A doctor walked into the room where the police and Jonathan were talking and said, "there's some activity on the EKG of the girl, is it your daughter sir?" He addressed Jonathan.

"Yes, is she OK?" He responded.

"She is stabilized and all her vitals are good, but she has sustained a traumatic head and possible brain injury. Comas are still an unknown area and there's no one treatment. It's watch and see at this stage. But I did want to keep you policemen informed as you requested. She is still far from having visitors, but we're hopeful." The doctor said with compassion in his voice.

"Thanks doc," Aaron said as the doctor walked out of the room.

Back in ICU Nicole's mind lingered in a nebulous condition as she tried to will herself back into consciousness. Her eyes started fluttering, her hands twitching while the doctors started speaking to her in gentle tones. Nicole then opened her eyes and moved her head toward the doctor. She attempted to say something but her words only came out garbled. Then Nicole was out again.

"It appears to be a lucid interval, and she has some clear fluid coming from her nose, it could be cerebrospinal fluid. We're going to need close observation on her all night. Her basilar skull fracture may have caused some tearing of the sheath surrounding her brain, so we want to watch for secondary brain infection. As soon as the neurologic surgeon comes in tell him we need a brain scan run on her to get a better assessment of her coma." The doc said with concern.

"She's young and beautiful, what a shame." The nurse murmured.

The brain scan was completed and it came back moderate. The medial team left and a nurse sat down in a chair next to Nicole. Her heart went out to her because she looked so much like her own daughter. She prayed quietly for her throughout the night.

Jonathan was now asleep after being medicated, the two policeman went back to the station once they were replaced with a patrolman who sat outside Jonathan's room.

The mother, Coco, had finished her medical exam, blood was taken and she was now asleep out of sheer emotional exhaustion. The doctors were fairly certain that she was an addict of prescription drugs but also was suffering from mild shock. They didn't feel she was suicidal but wanted to keep her at the hospital for the evening.

At 5am Nicole gently opened her eyes and darted a look over at the nurse who was now making notes on a chart. She could feel the neck and spine splint. "Where am I?" Nicole said.

The nurse was startled and replied, "You're at Saint Mary's Hospital, you've sustained a head injury during an accident at your house and were brought here last night. Do you remember any of that?"

"Vaguely," Nicole said. And then she fell back asleep. The nurse called Doctor Michael the neurologist, and told him what just happened with the patient. He said he would be there in a while but just to keep an eye on her. He was encouraged that she had gained consciousness twice in the past 8 hours and that she was coherent the second time, she seemed to be waking up.

By 9am Jonathan had been examined by the resident doctor, the bite marks required a number of stitches and they needed cleaning again with more antiseptics. The nurse replaced the dressing on his leg after the doc had a look at the knife wound. There was no infection in either the leg or face which made the doc happy. However, Jonathan found it much more difficult to speak as his face was swollen from his daughters attack. The doc warned him that there may be some scarring around the nose and his right cheek but plastic surgery had come a long way and it could be remedied.

But a bigger problem was brewing, Jonathan needed a drink. He had become a social alcoholic over the years and he generally started drinking by 10am in the morning. He could feel himself getting jumpy, irritable and emotionally volatile. This made him even more nervous because he didn't want the police to question him in this condition. They would become suspicious and may attribute his alcohol problem with the cause of last night's incident.

As time went on his head started pounding, his palms became sweaty, his heart rate went up and his eyelids were moving abnormally. All of this added to his agitation. He was wiping the sweat off of his palms when the doctor came to give him a final release from the hospital. When he looked at him he said, "your pupils are dilated, let me have a look at the medication your on."

"I'm OK doc, just a reaction to the traumatic experience I guess." Jonathan said.

"No, your palms are clammy as well and you're looking pale." The doc responded as he placed the stethoscope over his heart. "And you heart is racing." Are you experiencing any headaches, nausea or anxiousness?"

"I'm fine doc, except for this hole in my leg and a lacerated face." Jonathan said with a reassuring tone.

"Are you a heavy drinker sir?" The doc inquired

"Do you mean, do I love a drink now and then, absolutely. But if your implying that I'm an alcoholic, nothing could be further from the truth." Jonathan asserted.

"It looks like you're going through withdrawals, we need you to be honest because we can give you barbiturates to help you through the healing progress. Agitation will only prolong the healing of your facial wounds and could cause further tearing which will result in more scaring or possible infection. I'm going to get your blood results in a few hours so you may as well tell me now." The doc insisted.

The policeman was listening to the conversation and chimed in, "we're going to need a copy of the blood results as well doc."

"You'll need to liaise with the administrator, he handles all communication with the local police. But there shouldn't be a problem. We have always cooperated with the police." The doc said.

Jonathan felt trapped and he knew the investigators could use his blood alcohol levels as motive for the incident last night, his blood workup would prove he was loaded . "Yes, I'm a heavy social drinker and I could really use a drink right now."

"Hospitals are not bars that give out drinks, but I will give you some medication to calm you and help you over the withdrawal symptoms you're experiencing right now." The doc said with empathy.

The policeman stepped out of Jonathan's room and made a call to Philip the lead detective in charge of the case. "Philip, this is Aaron, the policeman down at Saint Mary's hospitals watching Jonathan. I've just learned from the doctor here that Jonathan is a heavy social drinker and it looks like he was intoxicated last night, which obviously could contribute to one of the reasons why the incident happened. I'm going to be getting the blood report in a few hours and I'll bring it over to you. You should also know that last night we learned that he is planning on leaving the country for good; he's been assigned to Geneva, Switzerland. We could be looking at a fight case."

"Good work Aaron, thanks for keeping me informed." Philip said with a smile on his face. *Now we're getting somewhere*, he said to himself. "One of you must remain with him at all times until we get him down here at the police station."

"Right, sir." Said Aaron.

Philip's phone rang, it was Lake. "Philip, I've discovered something that is disturbing and I think you ought to see this for yourself."

"I have a million things happening down here Lake, the girls mom, Coco is being released this morning and the two policewomen are taking her down to the police station for questioning. Do I need to come right now?" Philip vaguely argued. "And where is it you want me to come?"

"I'm still at the house of Jonathan, I've been her all night even though the team left about 2am. "You're not going to believe what I found sir." Lake insisted.

"Alright, I'm on my way but this better be good or you're going back to walking the beat in Alaska." Philip said annoyed.

When Philip walked into the secret room he was indeed impressed with the detective work of officer Lake. "You weren't kidding were you Lake, good work. Was it boredom, curiosity or good old fashion police work that led you to this room?" Philip asked.

"All three sir, boredom started the process, curiosity keep me looking and my police training alerted me that I was onto something." Lake replied.

"I might have to recommend you for detective training, Lake, would you like that?" Philip asked.

"My dream job sir, my dad was a detective in Los Angeles and I loved the stories he would tell at our dining table every night." Lake responded.

I want you to get our computer forensic investigator and tell him to met us here NOW! Something is a foot Watson and I want to know what it is before I question the man and woman today." Philip stated.

After their computer man had examined the computer files and once Lake and Philip had perused through the hard files that were there, they discovered that Jonathan was a major investor in diamonds. There were certificates and warranties from the World Jewelery Confederation, along with invoices, shipping manifests and mining shares. But the accounts were proving very difficult to hack into, the encryption was very sophisticated, plus it was asking for a message authentication code.

"Somebody doesn't want us in those files, call the FBI and tell them this could be an international diamond criminal case and we need a top computer hacker. That will get them interested." Philip said. While Philip was talking to the computer man Lake had been moving the furniture around and found a floor safe underneath the throw rug.

"Sir, here's something else you want to see." Lake called out.

"I'll bet you a hundred dollars what's in this safe Lake." Philip said with a smile on his face.

"I'm sure to lose that bet sir because I've got that female tingling sensation myself." Lake retorted with glee. They both looked at each other and said, "diamonds!" Philip said with a smile on his face, "and Jonathan wanted us to think that he is as clean as a plastered saint, ah."

Philip called a friend of his, the number one safe expert in Danton, and asked if he could come down immediately to help him on a case. It was going to be 45 minutes before he got there. He also called Jake, his detective in training, and asked him to bring Coco to her house, they would question her here.

Within the hour the house was swarming with FBI, safe crackers, computer experts, police to carry all the stuff to the station for evidence, forensics officers and photographers. And guess what was in the safe - diamonds. Over 8 million dollars worth of cut diamonds. They had also cracked his accounts and it looked like smuggling from the surface. But the evidence was mounting, the house on the computer screens was his place of business, the men and women were his crew and it was in Geneva, Switzerland. The certificates and warranties were all forgeries and the accounts were tax free. No wonder he was planning on leaving the country.

"Lake", Philip said, "look what you started here, this is going to make State news tonight and you're going to be the envy of every police officer, so be humble and thank everybody else for their part in this as well, understand?"

"Yes sir, we're a team." Lake responded.

"Good, now lets get all our facts together and interview the family, if that's what you can call them." Philip said. "You know, Lake, Jonathan would have gotten away with all of this if his daughter had not attacked them last night, the one thing he didn't see coming. Oh the irony of life. We got lucky on this one Lake."

When Coco and Jake entered her house, Jake called out, Detective Philip, we're here. Philip and Lake came up out of the secret room, the library and met them in the entrance.

"What are all you people doing in my home, Coco asked.

"I'll answer that question if you'll answer one for me, are you familiar with room behind the bookshelf in your library?" Philip asked.

Coco looked beyond the two of them and stared at the open bookshelf, "you're saying there's a room behind that bookshelf?" Coco inquired.

"Yes, ma'am. " Lake responded.

Coco walked around the two of them and went down into the secret room. She held her hand over her mouth and gasped, "What have you done Jonathan?"

"So you know nothing about this?" Philip suggested

"No, I've never seen or even imagined that this room existed." Coco said with astonishment. "What has he been doing down here and what are all these computers for, is he watching someone?"

"We would like for you to come down to the police station now ma'am, we need to talk about the incident of last night with your daughter. You can go upstairs and change if you would like, it's been a long night for all of us, we'll wait for you down here." Philip said.

"I should have know my husband was living a double life, he never tells me anything and he's gone to Europe so much of the time, but he has been a good provider. I guess money has a way of causing us to look the other way, right Mr. Detective?" Coco asked.

"Unfortunately, that's often the case. Philip replied.

# CHAPTER 13

# THE JESSE INCIDENT

*"Anyone who intends to come with me has to let me lead. You're not in the driver's seat; I am. Don't run from suffering; embrace it. Follow me and I'll show you how. Self-help is no help at all. Self-sacrifice is the way, my way, to finding yourself, your true self.*

*Matthew. 16:24 MB*

Catherine's dad was in his study working on a campaign speech and had agreed to see Catherine later that afternoon. At 3:30 Catherine gave Jesse a bell, (she had sweet talked his phone number out of a student in the university administration office who owed her a favor) hoping beyond hope that he was available to see her this afternoon as well. Jesse's mom picked up the phone in the hallway saying, "hello, this is the Reynolds" . Catherine said, "This is Catherine Stones, is Jesse home, can I speak with him." Oh hi Catherine, this is Jesse's mom, I remember you from years ago. He is home, I'll call him. "Jesse", his mom shouted, "there's someone on the phone for you, I think you want to take this one." She said with a smile on her face. He had just ended his shift at Speciality Cycling and had just arrived home, he was upstairs praying about the prophecy he had received on Sunday. "Coming mom." Jesse ran downstairs, took the phone from his mom and said,"Hello? "Um, hi. Jesse. This is Catherine Stone from .... school, and we met the other day in the drug store." She tried to make her voice sound sweet, but it just sounded shaky. Despite her pre-conceived idea of Jesse, she was actually nervous to speak to him.

"Yeah, of course, you have emerald eyes." Jesse answered before he could shop himself. *Why did I say that?* Jesse thought.

" O... um, thank you, how did you know that?"

"That's what everybody says," Jesse quickly replied.

100

Catherine caught herself thinking, *and what else are people saying?*

At the same time Jesse was thinking, *is this who I really think it is, or am I just hearing things?*

Catherine went on, "... Hey, listen, I'm planning the Young Leaders Sports ceremony and I heard that you were on the gymnastics team."

"Yeah, for four years." Jesse replied.

"Well, I thought it would be cool and different if we had some acrobatics along with the cheerleaders doing their thing as part of the program. Does that sound like something you'd want to be a part of?"

*I'd be part of dancing with obese old men if that's what you wanted,* Jesse thought, but instead he said, "Yeah, sure. That sounds *boss."

"Great!" Catherine said. "So, if you're free, do you think you could come over to my house in, like, an hour and we could plan it together?"

Jesse couldn't believe what he was hearing. "Be there in an hour." he said.

They said goodbye and Jesse took a moment to let everything sink in. His heart was *cranked, it felt like it had never beaten so fast. He ran upstairs and took a shower. In the mirror, he checked himself for any pimples and then brushed his teeth. He put on his favorite Jeans, mustered socks, his black shoes, a green shirt with his college jacket and bounded out the front door, laughing at himself for doing the exact same "hyper" thing his sister had done just weeks before. He suddenly remembered Nick, ran back into the house and gave him a bell.

"Hey Jesse, where are you? We were supposed to meet after your shift at work." Nick questioned.

"Nick, you're not going to believe this but Catherine called me and wants to see me at her house. Can you believe it?" Jesse exclaimed

"Well actually no, sounds a bit suspicious to me. You know she's a manipulator, aren't you a bit suspicious? Nick asked.

"What can I say, I'm a rabbit caught in the headlights." Jesse expressed with feeling.

"Well, I just hope I don't have to pick you up after making a *goof of yourself. Call me later and let me know what plans she has for you, OK?" Nick asked.

"I'll see you later." Jesse shouted as he ran to his car.

Jesse jumped into his Rambler and raced to her house. Jesse just passed a black Chrysler and thought what an awesome car it was, than he parked just in front if it because it was a ways from Catherine's house. He didn't think his Rambler would look right parked next to her pink Thunderbird . Meanwhile Catherine was telling her dad in the downstairs study that she was pregnant and the guy who took advantage of her was on his way over to talk to him. "Yes, Daddy, I'm pregnant," she said as he stared at her openmouthed.

Her father blitzed her with questions. What do you mean he took advantage of you? Did he rape you, did he get you loaded , did you lead him on, when and where did this happen, how old is this student?" Questions Catherine had not thought of before. She was realizing how many holes there were in her lie. She broke into her dad's tirade.

"Dad, I'll answer all your questions later but I'm a bit tender right now and Jesse is on his way over." Catherine intonated with uneasiness in her voice, and then started crying to masquerade her flawed story.

Jesse walked up the driveway and rang the doorbell. Jesse's hands shook as he waited outside on the porch. After a moment, a maid let him inside, led him through the foyer, and announced him. Then she moved away.

He recognized her dad, the Governor, but he looked like he was having a *cow and Catherine was standing with her hands covering her face, crying.

The Governor moved toward Jesse and shouted. "Young man, or should I say dipstick, scoundrel, or better yet, hypocrite. Did you do this to my daughter?"

Jesse's heart leaped into his throat. "Do what, sir?" He felt the sudden need for a bathroom.

"Don't play games with me." The Governor yelled. "I'm a politician. I invented games. Did you get my Catherine *knocked up? The Governor used that word to make his point that it was all Jesse's fault." He gestured towards his daughter.

Jesse felt like he'd been punched in the stomach and suddenly knew he was getting a *snow job. "Wh - what?" he said. He looked at Catherine in bewilderment, but she kept her face carefully covered. Jesse stood there frozen while her father was shrieking, screaming, yelling and hurling abusive words at him. It was a maelstrom of chaos. The first thing he felt, of course, was confusion, then shock, followed by hurt and anger. But after that, as the Governor accused him of this horrible thing, he began to feel something else. He watched Catherine as she sobbed. He could see her tears, which were certainly real. Something had made her do this. Something had made her afraid to tell the truth. And to his surprise he began to feel compassion and even pity for Catherine, this spoiled, rich Governor's daughter, the teen queen, this beauty who had never even glanced at him. She was scared. She was human. On one level he could sense the injustice of being used and *shafted by the girl he had liked, even envied at times. But this feeling of compassion seemed to eclipse all those emotions.

"Are you listening to me young man. You're in a lot of trouble!"

"I'm sorry, Mr. Stone," Jesse answered him, finally able to speak.

Catherine looked up for the first time, surprised, forgetting herself. "What did you say?" she said.

Her father ignored her and glared at Jesse. "You're sorry? You bet you're sorry." The Governor walked back behind his desk where he always felt he was speaking from a position of authority, "You Christians are all alike, telling us we're sinners and then you do something like this? You're all such hypocrites! He turned toward his daughter. "How far along are you, Catherine?"

"Eight weeks." she answered. She had no idea what was going on in Jesse's head. *Why did he say he was sorry?* She thought.

The Governor let loose with a string of abuses. "Oh, the papers are going to crucify me," he said. "And the election is fast approaching in November, then the Democratic committee from Washington, Catherine! How could you do this to me?" She began crying again, more softly this time. Everything was ruined. "Daddy, I can't even start - "

"Actually," her father interrupted, "this might not be so rough. A grandchild...a grandchild could make me into even more of a family man if I handle it right! The papers would eat it up, the public would love it. This could be fantastic publicity, don't you think so, darling?" His whole tone changed.

Jesse could only stand there, listening to them. He had no idea what was happening. He felt as if he'd stepped into a theater and begun watching a play.

"Daddy," Catherine answered, genuinely alarmed, "this is about me and my life, not your election or publicity."

"This is about all of us now, Catherine." He answered.

Catherine could see that her dad was acting the part, and this could only mean one thing. It was going to end badly.

The Governor spoke, with penetrating eyes he looked at his daughter and Jesse. "You two got yourselves into this mess and you two are now going to do the right thing to get out of this." He pointed at Jesse. "You're going to marry my daughter, young man."

"Daddy!" Catherine gasped, "you're talking about my future!" Her plan was suddenly backfiring on her. She shot a look over at Jesse, who looked like he was going to collapse, but his eyes, she felt her soul was being weighed by him.

"What's your name, son?" The Governor asked.

"Jesse Reynolds," he answered automatically. He would have thought he was watching a TV show where the script had all been written for him, except for the fact that he was not an actor and this was happening in the Governor's office, in Danton.

104

Catherine was searching for an argument. She was completely shocked at her father's reaction. Terrified, she stammered, "I....I can't marry him!"

The Governor abruptly turned into Catherine's father, "Baby, this is what happens when you're careless. This is the consequence. I thought I'd taught you better, but I suppose not. But I also taught you to make the best of things, and that is what I am doing with this situation. I am using it, not because I'm insensitive or greedy, but we all have to think not only of ourselves but also of mom, the two families and the good people of this State. This happy marriage of my daughter and a coming grandchild will be an example to the community of my good family values. We won't say anything of the child just yet, we'll wait till after the election and let it naturally happen in the course of time, say, months from now. You can see that, can't you Catherine?"

"I can see how you're using me," Catherine snapped. "I just can't believe you're doing this to me. I'm your daughter. Look at him, daddy. He's a Christian!"

The Governor thought of the irony of this situation. Of all the people on planet earth, he never could have imagined that a Christian would lead to his downfall. He was always so preoccupied with his political rivals and opponents that he didn't see this coming. And now a Christian was standing in his office, it was like red to a bull. He thought, *how could a Christian come to determine my fate? What is the Democratic committee going to think of this, and they will find out? It will be impossible to keep this quite.* Then like a flash of genius he said, "hmm, a conservative in the family, that may swing some of them over to my side. It will show that I'm tolerant, bipartisan."

"Ugh," Catherine moaned. "You're heartless!"

"On the contrary, this is big heartedness." The Governor said as he turned to Jesse. "You're going to marry my daughter, aren't you? Being a Christian you're supposed to do the right thing, right?" The Governor asked assuming he knew the answer.

While all the bantering was going on between Catherine and the Governor, the words of his mom that she had spoken many time came back to his mind. *God has a plan for you and your life, and when the right moment comes, you'll know who the right girl is.* Jesse had heard many sermons on faith but in his wildest dreams he never could have envisioned this. Was this really God speaking to him to marry Catherine. Was this the prophesy coming to past? It was obvious that he was being crucified for something he didn't do, but that was exactly what Jesus did for him. Was this to be his cross, the girl he thought he liked? His emotions were swirling, his mind reeling, but in his spirit, in his inner being he felt complete peace. It was like Shadrach, Meshach and Abednego standing in the fiery furnace but not being burned because Jesus was standing there with them. Or Steven the martyr, when the crowd was stoning him his face shone like an angel because of the presence of the Lord. That's what Jesse was experiencing, the presence of the Lord, even though he was standing in Nebuchadnezzar's den, the Governor's office, being stoned. Jesse felt undone, his life lay bare as a baby lying naked on a blanket. Yet in this moment of vulnerability he was not afraid.

Jesse looked at the Governor and then at Catherine and said, "I'll marry her, sir."

Catherine was horrified. She couldn't believe what was happening in her father's study. Why hadn't either of them reacted the way she'd planned? Why wasn't Jesse defending himself at all? Was he completely stupid , or was he playing a game of his own?"

The Governor smiled and nodded at Jesse and said in a fatherly tone, "now, what I don't want is any mention of this pregnancy to anyone. What we're attempting to do here is keep this out of the papers and prevent a scandal for everyone concerned. We'll tell the public that you had a whirlwind romance and couldn't wait to get married. Then once your married I'm sending you to England to go to university there until you've graduated, and by then the baby will be a couple of years old. I'll be a senator and the news of a grandchild will be just in time for the beginning of the next election. Your wedding and the child can be a political double-header. As Reinhold Niebuhr said, *"God grant me the serenity to accept the things I cannot change; Courage to change the things I can; And wisdom to know the difference."* That's what we're doing here Catherine, when life gives you lemons you make lemonade."

Catherine could see why the Democratic Party was inspired by her dad, she could see his worship of power was influential, brutal but galvanizing. Unfortunately she was the casualty of his political engineering.

"Governor," Jesse interjected, "I'm going to have to tell my parents and a few other people who know that Catherine and I have not been dating the truth, but I believe they will be discreet. I'll have to get back to you on their reaction and what they're willing to live with. This is going to be a colossal shock to them as well."

"You just remember young man, you're the reason we're all in this mess, and if you think you can live with destroying our lives and future, I'll become your worst nightmare. Do I make myself clear Jesse? All I ask is that nobody talks to anybody unnecessarily until we have a strategy and we're all on the same page. Together we go down with the ship or together we succeed. We are on the edge of an immense decision so proceed with caution." The Governor responded with an elevated voice.

"I do want to do what is right here, Governor, and I can only say how sorry I am for the awkward situation you are in. I except the blame and will do what the Bible says, "love covers a multitude of sins." Jesse said reassuringly to the Governor.

"Well, you should have done what the bible said eight weeks ago, then we wouldn't have to be covering anything up. This is my only daughter, I'm not just a politician, I'm a father as well, and you have violated my honor, my family and my most precious possession." The Governor shouted, and then the unseen was seen, the Governor, Catherine's dad began to cry. He buried his head in his hands sobbing, his anger was spent, and his love for his daughter finally reached his consciousness.

Catherine was stunned. She had never seen her dad cry, he had always been the rock of Gibraltar. And Jesse admitting guilt and accepting the blame. The weight of her decision now collided with her self serving scheme. Her veneer was cracking and she didn't like what she was seeing underneath. Maybe Nicole was right, this was a monstrous plan.

"Could you give us some privacy Jesse, I want to talk to my daughter alone, and you need to see your parents." The Governor choked out.

That was all Jesse needed to hear. He got himself away from that house as quickly as he could. During the drive home, all he could think about was, did that just really happen? Did I just hitchhike a ride on Sputnik? Am I someone's fiancée? Am I really going to marry Catherine Stone? He couldn't think. He prayed. He realized that by marrying Catherine, he was admitting to everyone that he had done something wrong, something that he didn't do. "What am I going to tell my dad and mom, my youth pastor, the church, my friends, myself?" It was overwhelming. He prayed again. "Is this your plan for my life, God, to have my reputation ruined, to stand there and take all the blame for someone else's stupid mistake? I'll become a silhouette, a shadow that will be seen against the background of shame." Unexpectedly the scene of Jesus hanging on the cross saying, "Father, forgive them, for they know not what they do," from the movie, 'Days of Triumph', ran through his mind . "Is this what true Christianity is, God? Is this what true love is? Suffering for someone else's wrong?"

Jesse definitely felt like a knife was being shoved into his heart. It felt so strange to go abruptly from almost no responsibility to this. As he reached his house, he felt like a stranger entering the front door and going up the stairs. He went into his room and threw himself onto his bed and prayed. Unexpectedly the prophesy from the evangelist Mary Sutton came into his mind.

*"God has chosen you, young man, to a Calvary path. You will be misunderstood by those closest to you, and criticized by people you thought cared for you. The Lord says, '"Like a lamb taken to be slaughtered and like a sheep being sheared, he took it all in silence.' That's what he asking of you, to suffer in silence and let God defend you. Your soul will die and be resurrected; you will fall and be raised by His right hand. You will only have His word and His Spirit to rely on, but His grace will be sufficient."*

The pastor and Mary were right. Nothing could have prepared him for this because this was apocalyptic. In the meantime the Governor called Andy and Jim and asked them to look into Jesse Reynolds and his parents. He told them this was top priority and could shape his political career. A second potential scandal in two weeks, what was going on?

# THE PARENTS

*"When his parents saw him, they were astonished. His mother said to him, "Son, why have you treated us like this?"*

*Luke 2:48 NIV*

Jesse waited for the second most important conversation of his life - this time with his parents. He was in his room praying and reading the bible, trying to prepare himself. He read Ezekiel 22:30 *"I looked for someone among them who would build up the wall and stand before me in the gap on behalf of the land so I would not have to destroy it, but I found no one."* Jesse knew that if he didn't marry Catherine there was a real possibility the baby would be aborted, or that the family would be *shafted by a scandal. This was the big leagues, it was not living a compromised Christian life or being a bystander, this was now trying to make sense of his faith in a real world where his theology would no longer fit into a nice neat package. Being true to the word of God, listening to the Holy Spirit, loving his family and doing what is right were all clashing and imploding at the same time. In the end it was this strong sense of witness he had in his inner most being that the prophesy and the leading of the Spirit was the right course of action. Plus what the bible said about why Jesus had to die on the cross. Suffering for our sins and not His own.

Jesse went to his drums and thrashed out his anger with loud, driving beats. Tears flew from his eyes landing on the drum heads and splashed about as he pummeled them. His soul cried out through his drumsticks, clanging his theology on his cymbals, driving out his confusion through his percussions. This was where he could pour out his pain, his heart, his confusion, where emotional eruptions were released. He slammed his drumsticks on his mid Tom, drained. "Just because I like pushing myself in sports doesn't mean I like extreme Christianity," Jesse shrieked out. But there was no escaping God's call, every time he read the scriptures, the topic of suffering seemed to jump off the pages at him. His bible was open to 1 Peter 4 which read, "Beloved, do not think it strange concerning the fiery trial which is to try you, as though some strange thing happened to you; but rejoice to the extent that you partake of Christ's sufferings, that when His glory is revealed, you may also be glad with exceeding joy. " He was destined to suffer, just like so many followers of Christ were before him. It was inescapable. Trust God or run.

He sat through dinner distracted, trying his best to act normal. After dinner he asked if he could speak with his mom and dad privately. Amy, his little sister, had just been picked up to spend the evening with her friend. Jesse stood before them, wanting to savor these last few seconds before his parents would forever have a completely different view of him. He remembered how hurt they were about the drugs in London, but this was so much bigger, Jesse was afraid. "I don't know how to say this," he began, "but an unexpected... crisis has come up. Just today. Um, ...you know the girl I sometimes talk about, Catherine?"

His parents were nervous. They had never seen their son act like this before. Something serious was definitely going on. His mom managed to act cool and said, "Oh, yeah, the Governor's daughter, right? The Valedictorian?"

"Yeah, her," Jesse continued. His throat was dry. " Well, today I went over to her house, thinking we were planning a sport program. That's what she told me we were doing. But when I got there, Catherine was crying really hard and her dad was going *ape." He paused. "I'm sorry, but there's just no way to prepare you for this except to say it.. Catherine told her dad that I got her *knocked up."

There was an odd split second in which Jesse saw a wide range of emotions swarm over his parents' eyes. After the shock set in, his mother gasped and put her hands over her mouth saying, "Oh, no!" While his father could only ask, "Tell us this is not true, son."

Jesse shook his head, "No, it's not true, and I hope you believe me dad....... but something happened while I was there."

"What happened?" They said in unison.

"It's like.....It's like I had an *eureka moment with God.

"And?" His father said anxiously.

"I was standing there in the room with them, completely confused, with her dad shouting at me and Catherine crying... and the room was *cranked with emotion. And I mean, I've barely even spoken to this girl before. Then suddenly, I felt sorry for her. I realized she was lying to make herself into a victim, and I was her idiot, and as I watched her, this love filled my heart. I actually felt compassion for her, not anger. And then, Mom, your words came into my mind. '*God has a plan for you, and you'll know when that moment comes who your one true love is.'* You just said that the other week."

She spoke in a slow strange voice that Jesse couldn't remember ever hearing before. "Honey, but I didn't think I was referring to this kind of scenario."

"I couldn't have imagined this kind of situation either, Mom," Jesse answered patiently, "but Mom, I know God spoke to me. He filled my heart with His love."

"Wow, son, I don't know whether to laugh or cry," his father responded as he put his hand over his heart and sat down.

"Well, her dad told us that we had created this problem and so we had to fix it by doing the right thing." Jesse went on. He watched as his parents' eyes grew wide, knowing exactly what ' the right thing' meant. Jesse confirmed this by saying, "He wants us to get married soon.... and very soon."

"This is a nightmare," his mother cried. "You should have run out of that insane asylum the moment you were accused! We don't even know this girl or her family!"

"Mom, I couldn't leave! God was speaking to me," Jesse answered.

His father put a calming hand on his wife's arm and pulled her down to sit next to him, "*slimmer down, honey," he said. "Let him finish." Sitting down, she put her hands between her legs and bit her lip, then started rocking back and forth.

"Go on, son," the father said apprehensive.

"All I can say is that in that moment, I just knew this was God's plan and I was supposed to marry her," Jesse said.

His mother started whimpering. " Son, do you know what this will do to us as a family? We have to face Pastor Greg, the entire church, all our friends and neighbors. And have you thought about your sister, Amy? Not only will she be teased and bullied, but she's going to lose a lot of respect for you. She looks up to you. Why on earth didn't you expose her lies? We're going to have the word 'hypocrite' tattooed on our foreheads when this gets out."

Jesse interrupted, "Mom, I feel like an *odd ball, , and I know this seems crazy.... but Jesus didn't expose me, He forgave me. He willingly went to the cross suffering my shame, suffering the consequences of my wrongs. His reputation was totally ruined, but He didn't try to fix it. He took the fall for me, and I just felt He was asking me to do that for Catherine, and her family. I know I look like a *dipstick. . I can hardly believe this is me saying this. And I know I'm putting you guys and Amy in a very awkward place."

"Awkward? This is dreadful," Mom said.

"I'm not trying to sound all spiritual, but this is a chance to do something totally for someone else with nothing in it for me. To love my enemy, to turn the other cheek." Jesse choked out.

"But, son," his dad answered incredulously, "There's a big difference between turning the other cheek and marrying your enemy!"

The words hung stiffly in the air for a few seconds. Jesse knew his parents were going to be hurt by all this. "I'm so sorry," he said to them, " but if I don't marry her, she'll have an abortion, be branded by the newspapers and

113

the family will be ruined. But if I do marry her, God's love can shield her and her family."

His dad's eyes were looking down at the floor when he said, "Wow, son, what you're saying is your willing to be a living martyr? Because we can see from this that Catherine certainly has a cruel side."

His Mom was now crying, choking out the words, "Oh, Jesse, is this the life we raised you for? My heart is breaking for you, and for us. She doesn't deserve you."

"Mom, I don't deserve Jesus either. I hate that you and Dad have to share in my fate, but I'm going to really need you because this is either the stupidest mistake of my life or a moment when all of heaven will applaud my decision. I'm scared because you two have such a great marriage, and I've always wanted that for myself."

"This is a huge decision. You may regret this for the rest of your life," his father said as he got up and pulled the three of them together, than he put his arms around the family and said, "Let's pray." As dad began to pray his speech became slurred and slow, than he sloughed down to his knees with heavy breathing. He started vomiting, he became light headed and fell to the floor. Mom screamed, "he's having a heart attack, call 999 !"

Jesse called 999 and the ambulance was there in 14 minutes. Jesse's dad was lying on the floor wheezing and clucking his chest. Mom and Jesse were praying with tears pouring down their cheeks until the paramedics arrived. Guilt overwhelmed Jesse thinking that he had killed his dad with the news he shared with them. *How could this be God's will, how could he expect so much of me?* Jesse thought. His mom looked at Jesse with eye's asking, why?

The paramedics took Jesse's dad's heart rate which was dangerously high and shouted, he's having a myocardial infraction, and then gave him a shot of atropine. They connected him to a resuscitator

and put him on a stretcher. The mother went with them while Jesse stayed home because Amy was due home at 9pm from her friend's house. They decided it would be better for Jesse to talk to Amy in person rather than upset her on the phone and then have to arrange her wanting to come home early.

# CHAPTER 15

# AN EVENING OF CALM

*Rest assured that justice is on its way and every good heart put right.*

*Psalms. 94:13 MB*

Jesse's dad, Sam, was rushed into heart surgery while a junior doctor was explaining to Jesse's mom, Shelley, the treatment of catheterization, a procedure where they inflate a narrow balloon into the clogged artery to clear it. To her relief the treatment went satisfactorily and the dad was placed in the intensive care unit for observation. As Shelley went to sit down next to her husband she noticed the young girl, unknown to her, next to them.

It was Nicole, still in a coma. She was very thin and looked hardened, steely. Shelley wondered if Jesse knew her, she was about his age. Standing next to her was a man with a police badge, he was making notes on his pad. It was detective Philip, checking in on his star witness to see if there was any progress, but the nurse told him there wasn't. As he scrutinized her (a natural tendency from his years of profiling people), he thought, *she has a savage beauty about her. They say a mind is a terrible thing to waste, but to discard a life, especially a young persons life was criminal and cruel. How can parents abuse the one's they say they love.*

On the other side of Sam was a another young man who looked in his mid to late twenty's. His name was Glenn, he just arrived a few hours before because of a major car collision. He had just bought a new car, a Corvette, and was not used to the power of a super-car. His accident made the 6 O'clock news because it happened at the corner of a very famous intersection called Franklin's Corner. The four streets that led off of that intersection had all the major government buildings for the state. It was known as the

116

'fountainhead of power.' Now he lay in a coma with tubes coming out of his mouth. Standing over him was Senator Jackson, she recognized him from the papers and various news reports. He was with his aid as they inquired about his medical condition. She thought how young the two patients were and prayed for them as well as for her husband.

She noticed a Gideon bible beside her husband's bed and picked it up. She opened it to a random spot hoping God would speak to her and the words jumped out at her from Psalm 94:19, 'When the cares of my heart are many, your consolations cheer my soul.' She looked up and prayed, "I could use some consolation now Lord, my heart has been broken tonight. My son's being branded as a rapist and my husband is lying in intensive care. I feel all alone, how am I going to cope with the fallout of today?" She looked at the bible again and flipped the pages to Psalm 37 and read, 'Do not fret because of evil men...be still before the Lord and wait patiently for him; do not fret when men succeed in their ways, when they carry out their wicked schemes. Refrain from anger...the salvation of the righteous comes from the Lord; he is their stronghold in time of trouble. The Lord helps them and delivers them.' "That's exactly what I need Lord, help, if there is anyway you can turn this situation around I would be grateful. I have no one else to look to but you Lord, my family needs a Savior." Pastor Greg came walking in as Shelley just finished praying and spoke some comforting words and prayed for her husband. The pastor then noticed Senator Jackson and walked over to him, introduced himself and offered to prayer for the young man he was obviously concerned about. He put his hand on the Senator's shoulder and asked, a friend or your family?"

"My cousin, Glenn, he was always a little on the wild side and I've tried to keep an eye on him, but you can't save people who don't want to be saved, can you pastor?" Jackson said with sadness.

"You're right there Senator, that's why we pray and trust that God will save them, because we all need saving ourselves." Pastor Greg whispered back.

On another floor of the hospital was Jonathan, Nicole's dad, recovering from the knife wound. An armed patrolman was sitting outside his room because Jonathan was a possible flight risk as well as a target. When it came to high level smuggling of diamonds, the stakes were high. He lay fast asleep, sedated by the pain medication. Coco was back home since the police and the FBI couldn't link her to the diamonds nor to the cause of Nicole's injuries. She was just an eye witness to her daughter's dangerous condition. Lake, the policewoman, was staying outside her house in her squad car to keep an eye on her. Jesse was home with his *sis, Amy, and he was grateful that his dad came through the surgery with flying colors. Jesse's guilt subsided, but if his dad had died he never could have forgiven himself. He was happy for the distraction of his sis . She needed his attention because at the age of 14 she was weepy over her dad's health.

In New York, evangelist Mary Sutton arrived at her hotel after a full day seminar at 'Fully Alive Church'. She felt very impressed by the Lord to pray for Jesse all day. She fell to her knees once in her room and starting interceding, crying out for strength and mercy for Jesse and his family. She prayed for over an hour until she felt the burden lift. She sensed a peace in her heart that God had heard her prayers and Jesse would come through the suffering. She remembered the prophecy she had given him and he had been on her heart ever since.

Catherine was being comforted by her mom at home but was thinking about how she was going to explain the events of today to her friends. She knew Beth and Ann were busy writing their script for the movie they were wanting to film that summer but she hadn't heard from Nicole. Catherine was a little concerned about her loyalty from the comments she made at their last meeting. She could be unpredictable at times and Catherine's plans had already been derailed enough. Hanna wanted Catherine to give her a *bell as soon as she was free after talking to her dad, which is why Hanna had called several times but Catherine didn't have the stomach to go into it with her right now.

Her dad was back on the campaign trail in Hartonbury, speaking at the teamsters union. When the Governor heard about Glenn's accident he asked the two special branch men to look into the accident to see if it was suspicious or just recklessness on Glenn's part. The Governor was secretly pleased and wore a grin on his face for the remainder of the evening. Yet, if it was Jackson, he was a more dangerous adversary than he realized. He was hoping it was just an accident even though it was very convenient.

Ted and his girlfriend were home with his parents, and his mom, who is the Saint Mary's Hospital Administrator mentioned to Ted that one of his more recent friends, Nicole, was in intensive care at her hospital. She said it was from domestic violence and the police had been in and out of the hospital all day. It looked serious and the doctors were not sure if the poor girl was going to make it. Ted had only met her a few days ago at Hanna's house for drinks but found her distant. He was surprised however that she had attacked her dad with a knife, she is so thin that he didn't think she had it in her.

Jesse's friend, Nick, was driving home from his new job at *Saks Fifth Avenue which he took just to get the discount on their cloths after finishing summer camp with the kids. He had been trying to get a hold of Jesse all night and was thinking of stopping by his house to see what was going on but his mom called and needed some aspirin for her headache. He was hoping that his warning to Jesse didn't come to pass but the longer he went without hearing from him the more apprehensive he was. He was going to have to wait until tomorrow to find out what Catherine wanted and why his best friend couldn't call him.

So all was on pause for the evening, but the tempest that began over the past couple of days was brewing, and the tide of turmoil was about to escalate. Life was colliding with dreams and hopes, with plans and prayers.

Olivia was in her car outside of Catherine's house reading "The Fellowship of the Ring," by J.R.R. Tolkien. As she was putting it down she finished reading with these words,

'All that is gold does not glitter,
Not all those who wander are lost;
The old that is strong does not wither,
Deep roots are not reached by the frost.
From the ashes a fire shall be woken,
A light from the shadows shall spring;
Renewed shall be blade that was broken,
The crownless again shall be king.'

Olivia commented to herself, "sounds like a prophecy to me," as she started up her car to drive back to her hotel.

# CHAPTER 16

# THE HOSPITAL

*"...Whatever is now covered up will be uncovered, and every secret will be made known."*

*Matt. 10:26 GNT*

Doctors were running, nurses adrenalized, buttons being pushed, phone calls being made and people from all over Danton were madly driving to St. Mary's Hospital. Nicole, Jesse's dad, Jonathan and Glenn were all awake and cognizant. Lake and Coco, Jesse, Amy and his mom, Governor Stan, Senator Jackson and his aide, detective Philip and his two policemen were all racing to the hospital to talk to the four patients. In front of the emergency entrance the sirens were blaring, cars screeching to a stop and people walking into the lobby. They all arrived as though they were synchronized swimmers, in perfect timing.

Everybody had to wait in the lounge because the staff were discussing whether to move the four patients before they had visitors or to wait to see how they reacted to them. The doctors decided to leave them in the intensive care unit in case they had a relapse from the visitors. Governor Stan and Senator Jackson were nervous being in the same room together with Glenn as their common reason. They were both reading a magazine so they did not have to talk to each other. Stan looking at the article on USS Nautius reaching the North Pole, the first nuclear submarine to cross under the North Pole. And Jackson reading how a 14 year boy called Bobby Fischer just won the U.S. Chess Championship. Coco was edgy and fidgeting, glancing at the book, 'Baby and Child Care by Benjamin Spock,' and wonder why things went so wrong with her and Jonathan, and Philip was like a horse in the gate before the race. He was ready to bolt into action with his star witness.

They were all allowed in but for a limited time. Detective Philip, Lake, Coco and the two policemen gathered around Nicole. The other policeman brought in Jonathan, her father, in a wheelchair. It was about to all go down. Coco grabbed Nicole's hand and burst into tears, out of relief for her daughter's life and because she was beginning to experience some slight withdrawal from her drug addiction. Her dad sat in his chair relieved that he wasn't going to be charged with manslaughter and that his daughter was alive. It was a tense moment since nobody knew what the outcome of this conversation was going to be.

When Nicole looked at her dad's face it was like cataracts fell off of her eyes, she understood his face was a legacy of her father's abusive behavior to her. Then a smile came over her, he was now wearing the scares of her abuse, how fitting. Her face then went like a mirror reflecting the mood of the people in the room but nothing of herself. The detective could tell she wasn't going to talk, he had seen that look many times before. Here was a girl with years of abuse that had finally hit the wall of her parents selfishness. He saw that Nicole finally understood she was never going to get from them what she had so longed for all her life, acceptance, value, love.

"I need to talk to your daughter privately," Philip said to Jonathan and Coco, "we can't stay long so would you please wait in the lounge across the hall?" He motioned to his policeman and Lake to go with them while he questioned the suspect.

"I know this maybe difficult, but can you please tell me what happened at your house the other night. This is a serious matter and we need to get to the bottom of this." Philip asked.

"What's your name?" Nicole asked

"Sorry, I've been around your parents so much these past two days that I forgot you were not a part of our conversation. I'm Philip, the lead investigator in this case."

"So I'm a *closet case, that sounds about right." Nicole commented.

"You're not a case, Nicole, you're a young women, a daughter, a student and you have friends, your life matters to more people than you think." Philip interjected.

"I'm sorry, it's just that I'm seeing my life from a whole new perspective. It was my fault Philip, I attacked my dad with a kitchen knife. I just went wild, I guess it was all those years of hurt and anger, lies and rejection. I just went crazy with rage. He pushed me off of him in selfdefense. I suppose I'll end up in the *cooler now, a fitting end to my tale of demise." Nicole conjectured with resignation.

"No, your parents are not going to press charges, Nicole, and as strange as it may seem, parents do love their children even if they don't always treat them right. Remember, parents have issues themselves, and much that has happened to you is not your fault. Your going to discover this as this case goes on." Philip said with some mystery in his voice. "You rest now, the doctors said you had a nasty fall on your head. And thank you for telling me the truth. I didn't think you were going to speak at all for a moment there."

Nicole smiled and detective Philip left the room. She turned her head to see who was talking next to her, and she saw Jesse. She gasped loudly, "Jesse," Amy, Jesse and the mom all turned and looked at her through the half drawn curtain thinking something was wrong. Jesse put his head in between the curtain and asked, "is everything OK?" Nicole looked shocked. Here she was face to face with the student she was helping to destroy. Her shame welled up and she began to cry silent tears as she stared into Jesse's face. "Shall I call for the nurse?" Jesse asked as he saw her crying. Nicole instinctively reached up and grabbed his wrist whispering, "I'm sorry Jesse, I'm sorry."

Jesse's mom asked, "Is she OK son, should I call for the doctor?"

"Just a minute mom," Jesse leaned down toward Nicole and asked, "do we know each other?"

"No, but I'm a friend of Catherine's." Nicole said.

123

Jesse's face changed, he stood up, looked uncomfortable and said he had to get back to his dad. Nicole squeezed his wrist, "No, no, please, there's something I need to warn you about." Jesse leaned back down towards her to hear more clearly. "Catherine is going to accuse you of knocking her up, don't go over to her house." Nicole pleaded with her eyes.

"It's too late, that happened yesterday." Jesse replied with sadness. Horror covered Nicole's face, she was too late, her sins had found her out. She had become just like her father. She let go of Jesse's arm and rolled over to weep.

"Thanks for wanting to give me the heads up Nicole, but it looks like fate got the best of us both ." Nicole was overwhelmed with quilt and cried all the harder which brought a nurse in to attend her. Jesse was surprised by the compassion of this stranger and his heart went out to her because it looked like her problems were as big as his.

Jesse turned around to join back in conversation with his dad. His dad assured Jesse that it was not his fault that he had had a heart attack, and not to feel guilty over it. As a matter of fact, I remembered something I read by Amy Carmichael in her book, 'If'. She wrote, ""If souls can suffer alongside, and I hardly know it, because the spirit of discernment is not in me, then I know nothing of Calvary love."1 Shelley began to cry and Amy asked, "what are you guys talking about?" Sam continued. "It's now clear to me that he's asking you to share in his suffering for the benefit of others. I don't like it, I don't understand it but I'll stand with you son and forgive the Stone family as well."

In the next bed was Glenn who was surrounded by Senator Jackson, his aide, and the Governor. Glenn was not able to talk because of the tracheotomy, but he was alert. They had removed all the tubes but his throat was too sore to speak.

"So, what brings you here Jackson, do you know this young man?" The Governor asked. He was hoping to embarrass him knowing the game he was up to a few weeks ago.

"He's my nephew, Stan. He's always been a rapscallion child, but I've tried to help him whenever I can. You know, be the good uncle." Jackson replied. And how do you know him?" Jackson asked coyly knowing all along he was his bookkeeper.

"He was my bookkeeper a number of years ago, it was one of his first jobs out of university." Stan answered.

"I hear you're getting some help from Washington for your campaign?" Jackson inquired.

"How did you hear that Jackson?" Stan said smiling.

Oh, I have my spies just like you Stan, but I'm a bit surprised you need it because you're ahead in the polls by 9% still." Jackson indicated.

"You can never have too much money or political clout, we still have five months and I've heard that you have a new strategy in the wings ready to be revealed?" Stan questioned.

"I guess we both have our secrets, but I hope you had nothing to do with Glenn's accident, I understand he came to see you last week." Jackson divulged.

"And why would I have anything to do with his accident, he simply came to apologize for the public funds he embezzled when he worked for me. I guess he never told you that?" Stan countered. "Doesn't he work for you now?"

"In a way, we give him the odd errand to do every once in awhile. His parents abandoned him when he was just a child and he would have become a ward of the state if my wife and I had not stepped in. He ended up living with another uncle but I've been his protectorate and provider. I guess I see him as one of my kids." Jackson confessed.

Well, maybe you should be more careful with the type of errands you send him on in the future, it sounds like he could use a break given his history." Stan spoke judgmentally.

Jackson scrutinized Stan's face and observed his smug appearance. *He knows*, he thought, *which is why he never went for the bait. Now he's gloating over it.*

Stan walked out supremely satisfied and thought, *stew on that one Jackson. Round two to me.* As he exited the room, Jesse, Amy and Shelley tried to cram through the door at the same time. As they all touched in the doorway Stan's sense of superiority drained from his countenance, Jesse grimaced and his mom scowled at the Governor.

"Excuse me," the Governor said, and scampered down the hallway as quickly as he could.

"You better run you coward." Shelley quipped bitterly.

"You'll have your chance mom, we're all going to have to get together to talk about the future once dad is up and about again." Jesse said.

# CHAPTER 17

# THE AFTERMATH

*"And rain fell on the earth."*

*Genesis 7:12 NIV*

Sam came home the following day, and it was a tearful time for the family. They talked, they prayed, they cried together a lot. And in the end, his parents came through to forgive the Stone family. It was the most difficult for his mom. Even though she was the more spiritual one of the parents, the reversal of fortunes for her son Jesse was one hundred percent the opposite of what she had envisioned or believed for him her whole life. After all that prayer, all that believing, all that sacrifice, all those promises she was standing on to have her son's future sidetracked like this was beyond her faith. She understood the concept of Jesus taking our place for our sins and crimes, but to ask this of her son was heart-wrenching. She decided to do what Mary, the mother of Jesus, did, "to ponder all these things in her heart." Now she understood Mary so much better when Simeon said to her, 'And a sword will pierce your own soul too,' to see her son accused, convicted and punished for the sins of others. That same sword had now broken her heart.

The most awkward question was Jesse marrying a non Christian. The dad kept asking how this could be God's will when God clearly tells us in 2 Corinthians, " Do not be unequally yoked together with unbelievers. For what fellowship has righteousness with lawlessness?" This was a challenge to Jesse's conviction of what he believed he heard from God in the heat of the battle at the Governor's study. But they all acknowledged that Catherine did make a commitment to Christ 5 years ago at their church during a special youth event. Her life hadn't reflected her decision that night but only God knows the heart. His dad and mom had to trust the Lord that she was a Christian because they knew that God would never ask them to do anything that contradicted his word. What the Lord had shown Jesse that morning in his devotions was the faith of Abraham. How God had asked him to sacrifice his son (which clearly seemed to be against God's nature) but because Abraham did believe that God was good and that he keeps his promises; God would resurrect his son Isaac. This gave Jesse courage to believe that God would somehow resurrect this situation as well.

Throughout the day Jesse kept attempting to call Catherine but she ignored his calls and he couldn't connect with her. He didn't know what to do or if she had changed her mind and would call it all off. It was clear from the way the conversation went yesterday that she didn't want to get married, and was taken by surprise as much as Jesse was at the suggestion by her father. When he went over the incident in his mind it all seemed even more confusing. Catherine started out crying and timid but ended up angry and belligerent. And why had no one called him after such a sweeping accusation. It was all very strange.

Jesse went to see his friend Nick and told him the news. He was *burned, but he did say he warned him. Then he laughed and said Jesse must have subliminally put the idea into Catherine's mind. Even though he did mention that it was an extreme way to get a date. He hugged him, congratulated him and made some remark about Daniel in the lions den. He promised he wouldn't expose the Stone family but keep things to himself. They had to figure out what to say once the news broke that Jesse and Catherine were getting married so they wouldn't lie but could cover the situation with respect. It was delicate. But Nick agreed by telling others that he was totally surprised by the decision (which he was) and that they needed to talk to Jesse if they wanted any more information about his decision.

On the other side of town at the Stone's house Catherine refused to come out of her room because of the decision her father made yesterday. She was attempting to emotionally hold her dad ransom, make him feel the weight of ruining her life. But the dad eventually just left for the office in Danton which took the wind out of Catherine's sail. Once there the Governor called Steve Forger, the Chairman of the Democratic Party.

"Your daughter did what?" Steven shouted down the phone.

"She said she was taken advantage of by a young man named Jesse, and she's just learned that she's pregnant." The Governor reacted sheepishly.

"What is happening to you, Stan? When we met in the hotel you had been scandal free for the whole of your political career. And now in the past few weeks suddenly you have this bookkeeper and your daughter." Steven complained.

"I know Steven, the heat has been turned up, but Glenn's plot has been exposed and to give you some good news, he's in intensive care at the hospital as we speak. He had a serious car accident and is out of commission for awhile. So fate has dealt us an auspicious hand on that one. And I believe this pregnancy with my daughter can be used to our advantage in the long run." The Governor responded positivity.

"And how is that Stan?" Steven asked rudely.

"When I first heard this from my daughter I was furious myself, but as I thought about it fortune seemed to smile on me with the thought, this young man is a Christian, a conservative. He's everything I'm not, but if he marries my daughter than we could use him to broaden our appeal. We would be bi-partisan, in that we would be representing family values and religion. It would make me look like a populist, someone who is standing up for the interest of ordinary people. Plus a marriage would do wonders for my election. It's the feel good factor to lift the opinion polls. Of course we would need the spin doctors working overtime on this one." The Governor said excitedly

"You think so." Steven interrupted.

"I think an abortion would be too risky at this time when we're so close to the election, the papers would crucify me and my family. And because of when the election is, just before thanksgiving and the Christmas season, people are beginning to think about family and friends. Even though people know my liberal views, my conservative incumbent, Senator Jackson, would paint me as a villain.

"Are you saying to me Stan that you're willing to sacrifice your daughter's future and happiness to further your career?" Steven asked pointedly.

"We'll, I'm thinking of her as well. The scandal would ruin her as well as me, for any normal girl no one would take any notice, but because I'm in politics she will be front page gossip." Stan explained.

"I know all that Stan, but I must say, you continue to surprise me, you're more ambitious than I thought you were. Anyone who would throw his own daughter under the bus like this is presidential material. Stan, you do have what it takes. The big problem is containment." Steven voiced.

"I would like to meet with James, Joshua and your lawyer to work out the details, but I'm thinking that we will announce the wedding very soon and set the date one month from now. Then they will go to England for their honeymoon, but I'd like them to stay in England, go to Oxford University so they can have the baby in relative privacy after my election. Once in England there will only be two months to the election and hopefully all of the attention will be on me and the campaign here in America." Stan explained.

"It's a risky plan and there will be a number of loose ends, it's going to take finesse, misdirection of information and bluffing. We need to create a distraction, give reporters something to chase up while the wedding plans are in progress, let us have a think about that and we'll get back to you." Steven suggested.

"Thanks, Steven, for understanding and standing by me. I appreciate your continuing support and cooperation." Stan expressed.

"Keep your head Stan, don't let your emotions influence your decision and keep checking in with us, collaboration is best in these kinds of situations. Talk to you later." Steven hung up.

It was a very humiliating call Stan had to make. His anger at his daughter returned. Like rain falling on the earth peevish thoughts soaked his mind, thinking how imprudent, indiscreet, injudicious and foolish Catherine was to let this happen to her. His teeth were grinding as he thought of it. She should be sent away on an Amazon River excursion and made to live with the natives for a year, sleeping with the snakes. That might sober her up. Or maybe exiled to a Tibetan monastery where her head would be shaven and could only eat grass and drink goat's milk.

He slumped into his chair and gave a sigh of exasperation. Teenagers! Why did they do away with chastity belts, the middle ages were looking better all the time. But his exasperation turned into hurt. Tears rolled down his cheeks as he thought of his little girl, how innocent she was, how much she loved to please him. He remembered her shouting to him at the park when she was at the top of the slide, "Look at me, daddy." Then there was her first speech in junior high, her prom, the playful banter they would have around the dinner table. The kisses she gave him at breakfast, seeing her so excited as he drove her to school. He had always trusted her, believed in her, and then came Jesse. Boys! He stood up thinking, why am I so angry at my daughter when it's really Jesse's fault. He's not a Christian, he's the devil, a *scallywag. He's the one who should be punished. He's the one who should be sent to Siberia. But his anger subsided when he thought of Jesse going to the papers. Even with all his power, all his connections, he was forced to play ball. Who really is in control? How funny, one student of no consequence seemed to hold his fate in his hands.

# CHAPTER 18

# DIAMONDS, DIAMONDS

*"A fool finds pleasure in wicked schemes."*

*Proverbs. 10:23 NIV*

"You're under arrest sir," then the handcuffs went on. "You have the right to remain silent. Anything you say or do may be used against you in a court of law. You have the right to consult an attorney before speaking to the police and to have an attorney present during questioning now or in the future. If you cannot afford an attorney, one will be appointed for you before any questioning, if you wish. If you decide to answer any questions now, without an attorney present, you will still have the right to stop answering at any time until you talk to an attorney. Knowing and understanding your rights as I have explained them to you, are you willing to answer my questions without an attorney present?" Gilford the policeman said.

"Of course I want an attorney, and I'm not answering any questions until she gets here." Jonathan briskly retorted. When Jonathan stood up to be transferred into the wheelchair Raymond frisked him for any weapons.

Gilford, Aaron and Raymond followed Jonathan as a volunteer pushed him out of the hospital in a wheelchair. When he arrived at the exit doors he stood up, but needed a crutch to walk with because of the wound in his leg. The two policemen grabbed a hold of his two arms and helped him to the squad car. They opened the door, Andy put his hand on the top of Jonathan's head and pushed him down and into the backseat. Gilford drove the car while Andy and Raymond sat on either side of Jonathan. They were taking extra precautions because of the seriousness of the crime and the amount of money involved. Gilford was new to the force and was handy to have around because of who he was, Gilford Ames the third. His family had lived in the same house for three generation and were true New Englander's. This meant that they knew someone who knew somebody who knew someone. He was well connected.

At the police station he was processed, given an in-depth search, his personal items were removed (wallet, belt, watch, contents of his pockets) and were inventoried. He was then fingerprinted, gave his personal data to the booking cop, than Jonathan made his phone call to his lawyer and was then sent directly to an interview room for interrogation. The room was sparse with bright lights that hurt your eyes, with a cold metal table with two other chairs. There was a camera mounted in the ceiling with a recording device in the middle of the table. It was not what Jonathan was used to, he always stayed in a 5-star hotel, but this, this was a hovel to him.

Gilford, Andy and Raymond stood in the three corners of the room as Philip walked in. He threw the bag of diamonds onto the metal table making a loud thud.

The tie on the end of the bag came lose and several diamonds spilled out trickling onto the table, sparking, twinkling. Everybody's eyes widened but Jonathan remained motionless, expressionless.

"You're trying too hard Jonathan, anybody's natural reaction to seeing diamonds glinting in front of them would have responded with wonderment or delight. But not you, that's because you smuggle diamonds everyday of your life. Your non reaction just told me you're guilty as sin." Philip goaded him. Andy moved behind Jonathan from the corner of the room, a tactic to make Jonathan unsettled. Philip continued.

"Your face look's tender, you might be carrying some scars for awhile."

"Nicole was out of her mind, and I guess I might have deserved her anger, though this was a bit extreme. But to answer your question, diamonds are my business, they're legitimate, I have the certificates for them." Jonathan said smugly.

"You mean these certificates, and invoices?" Said Philip as he scattered them across the table.

"Yes, and what right do you have to break into my house and steal my personal property?" Jonathan expressed with indignation.

"Now, now, Jonathan, you're smarter than that, you invited us into your house the night of your domestic violence incident. Plus I have a search warrant here. Do you know what we've discovered Jonathan, your certificates and invoices are all forgeries. They're very good, you must have paid top dollar for them, but the FBI have all the latest technology and experts. The evidence is mounting Jonathan." Philip gloated a bit and enjoyed having a bit of lark* with Jonathan. And guess what else we have unearthed, our lip reader has been spending the last three days watching your people in Switzerland." Jonathan's eyes enlarged, his first reaction to the interrogation.

"I don't know anything about a home in Switzerland, or any people." Shouted Jonathan out of frustration.

"I didn't mention a home Jonathan, are you confessing to something? Philip smiled.

Jonathan's eyes went wild, he jerked his head back to get his thick black hair out of his eyes and asserted, "What difference does it make, I don't own a home in Switzerland anyway. It was just a slip of the tongue,"

"Would you like to see another piece of paper Jonathan?" Philip was now enjoying himself a little. "It is a deed to a property in Geneva, Switzerland. And guess whose name is on the deed? Philip waited for affect, wanting the tension to build so Jonathan would keep talking. "It's yours Jonathan, sole owner of a 3.6 million dollar home, only 20 minutes from the airport and only 8 minutes from the main highway. Very strategic spot I'd say, wouldn't you?"

Jonathan was sweating, he could see the police had more than enough to prosecute him. His only hope of escape was getting out on bail and fleeing the country. In Switzerland he would be safe and he would be wealthy, the $8 million of diamonds that they seized was only a tenth of what he had stored up in Switzerland.

"I want my lawyer, I'm not saying another word until she gets here." And with that Jonathan tightly sealed his lips, crossed his arms and stared at Philip. He was determined to give nothing more to the police. Philip could see that he was afraid, and for good reason, he was going away for a long time. Philip had the police escort him to a holding cell where he made his call to his wife Coco since his lawyer was already on her way over to the police station.

"Where are you Jonathan, there are police all over our house, and there's a secret room I never knew existed. What's going on?" Coco asked.

"I'll explain everything when I get home but they have arrested me and I'm at the central police station in Danton. I want you to listen to me very carefully, don't say anything to the police, the FBI or anybody who asks you anything. It could only damage my case. I swear to you Coco, I'm innocent." Jonathan voiced. "It's just a big misunderstanding, I'm a legitimate businessman and all my enterprises are above board and honest. For whatever reason they're looking for a fall guy. Can you keep quiet until I get bail and we can talk at home?" Jonathan asked kindly.

"First Nicole then you, why is this happening to us?" Coco asked.

I'm sorry about Nicole, have you heard anymore about her since we saw her last at the hospital? Jonathan replied.

"She's recovering exceptionally well, the doctors are saying. She should be able to come home tomorrow, they just want to keep her there for one more night of observation."

"I hope to be home soon if you can arrange bail for me after the hearing at the courthouse. Then we can start picking up the pieces again and, I don't know, maybe we can all take a holiday and see if we can't find a solution to all of this. How about Paris, how does that sound honey?" Jonathan asked.

"Paris sounds like heaven about now Jonathan, I'll try to be at your hearing if Nicole is well enough." Coco said tearfully.

"Thanks hon, I know I said some mean things but Nicole is our main concern now, lets just put our differences aside and concentrate on our

135

daughter. Get some sleep...." and the phone went dead because Jonathan didn't have anymore change to put into the pay phone at the station. Dead, that's about how Jonathan, Coco and Nicole all felt at that moment.

CHAPTER 19

# THE DECISION

*"But I tell you not to resist an evil person. But whoever slaps you on your right cheek, turn the other to him also."*

*Mat. 5:39 NKJV*

The two families, the Reynolds and the Stone's, eventually had the fated talk. The air was filled with blame like a heavy fog on a chilly winter morning. Silent stares, rigid bodies, unnatural greetings with handshakes a little too strong to be comfortable. Sam and Shelley managed to keep their cool but Shelley did cry from time to time. The talk was held in 'The Governor's Study,' a room that imposed its will upon you. Books, congratulatory plaques, trophies, commendations - all the marks of someone important and threatening - the Governor. His wife didn't say much but stood there with a scowl on her face. It was right out of a Hitchcock thriller.'

The Governor started by asking everyone to call him Stan, "we all know how awkward this is for everybody and I'm sure you, Mr. and Mrs. Reynolds, are just as heartbroken and distressed about this as we are. Only we do want to point out that we're the victims here, and your son is the real culprit. He already knows how we feel so there's no need going into the 'what happened'. My daughter has explained this unfortunate, thoughtless, selfish...."

"We get it dad," Catherine broke in.

"Sorry, but I'm sure you can understand our outrage," Stan expressed. Jesse's mom began to sob and his dad looked over at Jesse with a last look of pleading in his eyes to end all of this with the truth. Jesse walked over and put his arm around his mom and held her. Catherine was mystified by their behavior, still wondering why they were all so compliant with her false accusations. Mrs. Stone just stood there with her arms folded, scowling at everybody. Daggers were in her eyes, infuriation written on her face and unforgiveness in her heart. She was feeling too scandalized to even enter the conversation because she knew she would sabotage the whole meeting.

Stan continued, "We are all affected by this premature pregnancy, our reputations, our careers, our standing in this community, our trust in one another, but I have never been one to cry over spilled milk. We have to look to the future and find a solution that will restore our fortunes. And as the Governor whose election for Senator is only a few months away I'm sure you must recognize how much this can damage my chances of being elected. I'm not saying that I'm more important than anyone else, but I do have the most to lose, and so I want to propose a plan that could work for all of us."

Catherine couldn't stand it any more, "you mean you want to save your hide."

"Absolutely I want to save my career, but I also want to save your future and the Reynolds any more embarrassment." The Governor shouted back at Catherine. "You forfeited your right to make the decisions regarding your future when you jeopardized all of ours. Now stop interrupting and let the adults talk here." Regaining his composure Stan turned to the Reynolds, "I'm sorry you have to witness this but as you can see my daughter is head strong and too much like me."

Sam spoke up, "I'd like to here your plan Stan."

The Governor stood up putting one hand in his pocket and gestured with the other one as he began to talk, which was more of a speech. "I propose that Catherine and Jesse get married in one month, and I'll tell you why. My wife and I do not want the baby aborted, (which was a lie, but an abortion would mean political suicide at this moment in his election), and we don't want everybody knowing about this pregnancy. It would ruin all of our reputations. We can simply say that it was a whirlwind romance and they wanted to start a new future together, which is partially true. We would then like to send them to England for their honeymoon, but they would stay there for at least a year going to Oxford University."

Jesse, his dad and mom all gaped with startled expression at Stan with their mouths open. Almost unanimously everybody in the room, except Catherine's mom, blurted out, "What?"

"Now just hear me out, I know this is a radical move but these are desperate times for us and we need to be thinking clearly and not allow our emotions to govern our decisions. The reason I suggest this is because they can enjoy the pregnancy and the birth of our grandchild, (which he said with maliciousness in his tone) in relative peace and privacy. If they want to come back after a year I'm sure we would all welcome that, but this way we can keep the press from sensationalizing this on every front page of the news. And they will, with me running for Senator. All of our names would be dragged through the mud but with them in England, married and going to university, it all looks legitimate." And Stan ended his speech with a serpentine smile on his face looking for applause, which none gave him.

"My dad, ever the politician, manipulating his words so everybody feels that they're benefiting when it's you who is the benefactor." Catherine snidely said.

"That's enough out of you young lady, your dad is trying to save your reputation, give you a future and shield you from a tabloid maelstrom that would break all of our hearts." Her dad snapped back.

"Stop being so selfish, you're acting like a child." Her mom blurted with shaky intonations. Her broken silence caught everybody's attention and they all looked over to see her face red with exasperated gall.

The tension was suffocating and the Governor took charge again. "I've already made arrangements with Oxford University for both Catherine and Jesse to attend. The applications, transcripts, recommendation and entrance fees have all been expedited through my office. I do have considerable influence in these kinds of matters, plus a healthy donation has accompanied the urgent enrollment. Meaning they have accepted them into their fall term.

Sam expressed concern because they were in no financial position to fund his son's university degree, especially in England. But the Governor made it clear that this was his plan and he was prepared to fully fund both their educational needs because of the political implication otherwise.

Everyone did see the reasoning behind the decision and it wasn't long before they were all in agreement. Jesse could see why he was the Governor. His logic was convincing, persuasive. Finally, the date of the wedding was set, the alibi established, and a happy ending predestined, until Catherine spoke.

"Dad, I can't believe you're doing this. You're ruining my life and any chance I have of becoming something." But her Dad droned on over the same plan again ignoring Catherine's outburst.

*Why are Jesse's parents agreeing to this? Hasn't he told them the truth?* Catherine ran out of the room and slammed the door. Jesse followed. Inside the Governor said, "Well, Reynolds, I don't want to seem ingenuous but welcome to our family!" But Stan's wife's body language betrayed his sentiment, her message was, 'over my dead body, we're family.'

"I think everything is going to be just fine if we keep our heads and don't panic!" He was masking awkwardness with his famous charisma, he could be crass from time to time, but he was a handsome man whose egotistical persona could be hidden with his charm. Jesse's parents sensed his duplicity but smiled with graciousness.

Out on the landing Jesse spoke to Catherine, "I'm sorry, Catherine, that you have to go through this." Catherine glared at Jesse, "What is your game? Are you after my dad's money, because we're signing a prenup so you'll never get a dime!" She was staring right into his eyes, only a few inches from his face and was stunned to see a look of sorrowful kindness. She faltered, startled, but quickly snapped back, "And don't think you're going to convert me. I believe in the god of me, myself and I."

"I'm scared, Catherine…" Jesse said,

"Scared?" Catherine spoke back. "I'm not scared, I'm *frosted. . This whole marriage thing is archaic, and why are you going along with this anyway?"

"I want to do what's right for you, the baby, your family, as well as for myself." Jesse gently pushed the words out of his mouth as if he was thinking of the words one at a time.

"You want to do what's right for me? Why? Wait a minute.... you know your not going to get into my pants and, by the way, don't think you'll ever touch me if that's your game. So, why?" Catherine said incredulously.

Jesse paused. "You're going to think this is—weird."

"This whole situation is weird." Catherine said.

"Okay, here goes," Jesse took a deep breath and said.... "I love you."

There was a slight pause. Catherine hadn't been guarded for that one. When she regained her composure, she smirked, "Oh, so you've been a secret admirer of mine? Out of 18,000 students I had to pick the one person who's been secretly stalking me. Now this is a twist of fate... it's unbelievable! Hollywood couldn't have come up with a better plot."

"It's not a romantic love." Jesse was quick to point out. "I mean, I like you. You're certainly a *knock out when you're not so *cranked up."

"Is this some kind of a religious, cult love?" Catherine asked.

"I know this sounds strange, but... it's just that I genuinely love you."

Catherine cooled her eyes again. "Listen to me, you don't want to marry me. I'm not going to be some *swell housewife. I'm not going to cook for you, clean for you, go to bed with you or watch your movies with you." Jesse only looked at her. She stared at him. *He has such tenderness in his eyes.* But the powerful women came back, she recoiled. "Don't try to call me, I'll call you if I want to talk." And then she turned around and walked off wondering how he could possibly love her after what she did to him.

"Now I know why I'm scared." Jesse said under his breath as he walked out the front door. Soon after his parents came out and they made their way home.

141

There were too many unanswered questions for Catherine. Why were his parents going along with this? Why has he not asked me who the father really is? For *pete's sake, are all Christians this easy to pull the wool over their eyes? She collapsed into her chair and sighed, "I'm too young to have a baby, to get married. I'm going to kill Ted!" She walked downstairs to grab her school books when her dad walked out of the study, Catherine said, "I can't believe you're actually going to make me go through with this, Daddy. I don't even know Jesse that well."

"That didn't stop you the night he got you pregnant," her father said. Catherine began to cry. She felt like all she did these days was cry.

"You're ruining any chance I have of becoming anything! A baby and marriage will take over my life. Do you remember what it was like to be 19, with a future?"

"I do remember, but I made good decisions, Catherine, I didn't do anything so STUPID. This one ridiculous mistake of yours could have ruined my entire career. All my life's work! We're lucky this boy isn't going to the papers, he could be making a lot of money on this story. The papers would love this. And we're lucky his parents are willing to let you two get married. All in all you're a lucky girl, and don't you forget it. I'm serious. I better not hear one more objection. Now, I love you. GOODNIGHT."

He left her standing in the lounge. Catherine had stood up while her dad was talking to her because she always felt vulnerable to his imposing will when sitting during his talks. Standing gave her a sense of equality, but today, standing did not equalize the battle of parental authority, instead she lowered her head and sobbed. *Lucky? I'm ruined.*

Catherine called her friends and asked them to come over that evening to share the ruinous news of her potential marriage. They had to all have a new cover story now that her dad had intervened with her plan. Hannah, Beth and Ann arrived, but no Nicole.

"Does anyone know where Nicole is?" Catherine asked.

"You haven't heard," Hannah said, "it's been all over the gossip circle." Hannah explained that Nicole was in the hospital just coming out of a coma because of a domestic violence row at her house. That her dad had been arrested, and their house was swarming with the *Heat and FBI. At one point they thought Nicole was not going to make it, but she's come through now. Nobody was able to visit her because the police had her protected and needed her for questioning.

"I've been so wrapped up in my own saga that I haven't thought about anything or anybody else. I feel horrible." Catherine sighed.

"Well, your situation is *boss, Catherine, but it is ironic, you tried to end a life and your dad, who we all would have thought to be a natural antagonist, ended up saving it. And Nicole, she has tenaciously hung onto her nightmarish existence and her dad almost took that from her." Beth, the story teller recited.

"Poor Nicole, we have at best only seen pieces of her soul, what she must have been living through all these years, for her own father to violently attack her and put her in the hospital." Ann voiced.

"Well we all know her father's a high powered alcoholic and her mother is addicted to meds." Hannah broke in.

"Most of the women in these upper class neighborhoods are pill pushers as well." Beth added with a laugh. "We look good externally but there's corrosion internally."

"I'm sorry to break into this moment of grief, but as you know my plan has backfired. My dad obviously believes that a marriage between me and Jesse is more politically advantageous." Catherine interjected.

"Then it's a good thing we picked a *Dreamboat, at least he's good looking." Hannah added.

"Good looks and beauty are like snow, they're appealing but can be inconvenient and dangerous. I know, because my self pursuit of flaunting and flirting triggered an avalanche of inflamed men, and these are the consequences. I wore the crown of campus queen, but I didn't realize that all crowns have thorns."

"Wow, you've become theatrical." Beth broke in, "getting knocked up is causing you to become serious."

"Sorry, I guess I am becoming a little melodramatic." Catherine went on to explain the story of what happened in her dad's study with Jesse, and how one unexpected turn of events lead to another, until her fate was sealed. Then she went over a sequence of plausible events that could have happened between Jesse and her which could have led to their marriage. It was a very loose story without exact dates or places so as not to get caught off guard when people pressed them.

As she finished her monolog she noticed the same Chrysler parked down the street again, and her anger erupted. "Look at this girls, it's the same car that's been stalking me for over a week now." They all crowded around the window to see this mystery car. "I've got a plan girls,"

"Not again, Cath," Hannah said with exasperation. "Your last one didn't go so well."

"I know, but I refuse to allow this woman to pry into my life, my situation is already at breaking point." Catherine said stomping her feet.

# CHAPTER 20

# THE ARREST

*"Agree with your adversary quickly, while you are on the way with him, lest your adversary deliver you to the judge, the judge hand you over to the officer, and you be thrown into prison."*

*Matthew 5:25 NKJV*

"Book him, we have all the evidence we need to put him away for a long time." Detective Philip asserted to Jake his trainee. To tell the truth Philip had had it with Jonathan's lawyer, a contemptuous, adversarial Cambridge elite who treated all police with disdain. She brought to Philip's mind a joke he had heard, "what's the difference between a Female Lawyer and a Pit Bull? Lipstick." Lawyers had made his job unnecessarily complicated and Jonathan knew how to pick them.

As Philip was walking back to his desk six FBI agents were striding towards him all dressed in their black suits, thin ties and *Monk comfort shoes. They walked up to Philip and handed him some paper work saying, "Our agents in Switzerland have been coordinating their investigating with the local police in Geneva and they have arrested those six people in the video feed in Jonathan's house. In searching the house they recovered another 8 millions dollars worth of diamonds in addition to the 6 million you found in his house. You stumbled onto a major crime ring that's global. America, Switzerland, South Africa, Holland, Germany and who knows how many other countries are involved right now. Your team has done a cracking job. But we'll need to take over the case now because it's an international ring of thieves we're dealing with."

"I was expecting this," Philip turned to Aaron and Raymond and asked, "would you guys get these gentleman the rest of the evidence we have on

Jonathan. This guy is good because there is no rap sheet on him at all. He has managed to keep himself under the radar all these years."

"We've arranged a pre-trial bail hearing at the courthouse this afternoon at 2 if you want to be there, we're hoping he doesn't get released on bail but is remanded in custody, but if not we're prepared with 24/7 surveillance."

"Yeah, I'll be there and we will inform the wife of the hearing, I'm sure she will want to be there."

"Thanks again for exposing this ring, you're top notch in my book, Philip. Hope we work together again. See you this afternoon. And speaking of the devil, it's Jonathan."

"You moved up into the big leagues now Jonathan," Philip announced. "Now you're dealing with the FBI, they ought to give your lawyer a run for her money." Jonathan was not looking so good due to the alcohol withdrawal, lengthy questioning and incarceration. They were accommodations he was not use too. The agents walked out with Jonathan in custody and Philip was a little sad not being able to see this case through, it was not his normal type of case and he had enjoyed the challenge.

* * * * *

That afternoon Jonathan and his wife, Coco, Detective Philip, the FBI agents and their lawyer were all in the courtroom to hear Jonathan's case. The prosecutor for the FBI was an experienced man with years of international criminal cases. He possessed a commanding presence, tall, well groomed, physically fit with styled black hair. He looked like he had stepped out of Forbes magazine. Jonathan's lawyer was fashionably corporate in a dress with shoulder length straight blond hair. She had a smile that said she knew something they didn't.

Jonathan's lawyer began, "Your honor, we request that our client be released on a reasonable bail charge, since we do acknowledge the seriousness of the charges, but our client is an upstanding citizen with no priors and he poses no threat to anyone sir. Plus there are special circumstances, his daughter is in the hospital due to a serious injury, and we believe he's been

146

unjustly accused of these diamond smuggling charges, and his wife is home trying to pick up the broken pieces of this tragedy."

"Your honor, we would agree, as the esteemed lawyer put it, that the defendant's home life is experiencing discomfort but unfortunately the discomfort he is suffering is directly due to his crimes." The prosecutor stated with concern in his voice.

"Alleged crimes, your honor." Jonathan's lawyer pointed out.

"You say alleged but we have overwhelming evidence that Jonathan Conrad is involved in an international smuggling ring that spans from here in the United States to Europe and to South Africa. The FBI and the Geneva police have already arrested 6 people, seized in total 14 million dollars in diamonds and the dates on the various certificates and shipping statements correspond to the dates of robberies that have been committed over the past 7 years, and we have only scratched the surface after one week of investigation. So because of the seriousness of the crime we ask the court to deny bail for fear of flight risk." The prosecutor implored.

"Your honor, there is no prior history that my client is a flight risk or dangerous, but rather a very successful businessman who owns and manages an international corporation. And as you can see for yourself, he is recovering from personal injuries and is walking with crutches. Now unless our esteemed FBI don't believe they can chase down a man on crutches then by all means incarcerate my client." Jonathan's lawyer entreated. There was laughter in the court until the judge hit his gavel on his desk.

The judge interjected, "I think you both have valid arguments, which means what we're looking for here is a little quid pro quo, so I am going to set the bail at $1,000,000.00 and we will set the trial date for one month from today. But I have a cautious caveat to this bail, your client is to under house arrest with police escort for extra security if he is released on bail. Agreed? Both lawyers said yes and Jonathan walked away with a malformed smile because of his injuries.

Later that afternoon Jonathan's lawyer transferred the money to the bails bondsman and he was free, except for the restrictions. Jonathan went home to find it taped off with yellow crime tape, his secret room in shambles and his wife, Coco, still crying. Jonathan was beginning to feel like a Chess piece on the board of his empire, which meant it was time to reverse this intolerable situation. He was feeling invigorated again, the rush of outwitting the FBI was intoxicating, which is why the life of crime appealed to him in the first place.

His wife ran to him, wrapped her arms around him and stuttered out, "your face, is that what Nicole did to you?

"She wasn't in her right mind hon, it looks worse than it is because the swelling hasn't gone completely down yet but the doctors said they weren't too deep and with some minor facial surgery I should be just fine." Jonathan assured her.

"What's going on Jonathan? I'm frightened. The police, the FBI, the secret room, all this talk of diamonds, what have you been up to?" Coco pleaded.

"You can see they let me out on bail because they're not sure if what they're accusing me of is true. Honey, I'm completely innocent. You know me, have I ever done anything that was criminal. Have you ever seen any shady characters around me? I'm not sure why, but I think they're looking for a fall guy for this international smuggling ring they keep talking about." Jonathan empathetically explained.

Coco looked up into Jonathan's eyes with her glance of dependency and sighed, allowing his words to marinate in her mind. "We're a mess, aren't we Jonathan?"

"Yes, we are hon," Jonathan responded "but we've known this for a long time. We're a toxic family which is why I wanted a divorce several nights ago, seems like a lifetime ago now. But we need to put this nasty business to rest for now, I have to get past this court case first, salvage my business and get our daughter home." All of which was music to Coco's ears.

"Thanks for not leaving Jon, I don't think my heart could cope with that right now." Coco murmured.

As Jonathan stared into Coco's eyes he could see her depression, her sadness and the tears stain down her cheeks from sustained weeping. Ever since she became addicted to meds she was given to emotional outbursts. "Why don't you go upstairs and try to get some sleep, while I clean things up down here, I've got a million things to do and they needed to be been done yesterday, OK?" Jonathan guided.

Coco made her way upstairs and Jonathan went to work hurriedly. In his library there was a second hiding place inside his metal globe that the FBI had not found. He turned the top half of the globe counterclockwise and it popped open, he lifted up the top half and inside was a suspended round globe with three buttons of different colors. He pressed each one in the right pattern and the top half of it sprang open and inside were several passports each with different names, a hundred thousand dollars, an open-ended airline ticket to Paris, France, an airport locker key and a small pouch of diamonds .

He called one of his accomplices, Kelly Walker, if that was her real name, and asked her to meet him on the 6 O'clock train to Lincoln, compartment H, seat J2. She was also to leave her rental car parked in row KK in the South lot of the Lincoln parking lot with the keys in a magnet box stuck under the car by the drivers door . He asked her to bring a package along with a five pound bag of fine salt. He looked out his window and could see the FBI agents in their black Sedan parked outside his house. He knew he only had one chance and the plan had to be perfect. He sat down in his chair because his leg was beginning to bleed from rushing around too much, but he wanted to take a moment for one last look because he knew he may never see his wife, daughter and the life he had known for so many years ever again. This was good-bye. The law had finally caught up with him and he couldn't imagine prison as a lifestyle for himself. He would rather be a fugitive with money. Besides, everybody in his world knew about his arrest, domestic problems and criminal charges of diamond smuggling, the Danton Chronicle made sure of that, he was their big news story. They had dubbed him, 'The White Collar Loki,' the famous Norse mythological shape-shifting, troublesome god. How was he ever going to live that one down.

He called Clyde and asked him to help drive him to the train station, but to come in through the backdoor with the car parked on the street behind his house. Clyde was a wizard when it came to electronics. He was his computer security connoisseur who had kept him under the radar all these years. After Clyde had driven the car around the back of Jonathan's house, he came in and helped Jonathan hobble out the backdoor with Clyde. They passed through his manicured lawn, out the back gate, through some shrubbery wrestling his way through because of his crutches, and into Clyde's car. As they drove to the train station Jonathan said his goodbyes to Clyde who had been his partner in crime for over 15 years. He instructed him to disappear for a while and was not sure when he would be able to contact him. They both knew this day could come and Clyde dropped him off with, "it was a good ride while it lasted, but just don't let them catch you again or we will all go down like dominos."

"Thanks Clyde, do you remember how we got into this, we met at that crazy conference called, "Change Your Future," and over coffee we were talking about buying something for our wives because we were in Miami, Florida and they were home with the children. And you said, diamonds aren't just a women's best friend, they're man's best friend as well."

"O yeah, because I thought diamonds would look good on my tie clasped."

"And I responded with, diamonds would look good in my safety deposit box. And that was it, an idea was born.

Clyde turned serious, "and now diamonds have us on the run, and run you better do to catch the train, Kelly is waiting for you."

Jonathan smiled and left the car with, "to the future than." He boarded the 6 O'clock train to Lincoln, made his way to the right compartment and sat down next to Kelly. He put his briefcase on the floor in front of him and picked up Kelly's backpack with the items in it. Kelly said to Jonathan, "I'm sorry, this seat is taken, my partner is joining me." Jonathan picked up his briefcase and said, "sorry ma'am." He went into the toilet where he jimmied the underarm pad off the top of his crutch. He opened the package and looked at the diamonds Kelly had brought him before pouring them into the metal frame of the crutch, then he poured in the fine salt to pack the diamonds so they wouldn't make any noise. There were several millions dollars worth of diamonds that he had been putting away as a nest egg for just such an event as this one. Than he took the small pouch of diamonds that he took from his globe and poured them in as well. He came out of the toilet, nodded at Kelley and lamely walked back through another carriage and disembarked. He made his way to Kelley's car, drove himself to the Windsor airport. When he went through customs the officer looked at his passport which read John Taylor and then asked, "What happened to your face, Mr. Taylor?"

"I know, it looks appalling, that's what I get for watching horror movies too many times." And the older officer laughed. "I tripped on the carpet in my living room and fell into my glass coffee table and the glass top shattered cutting my face and leg, you should have seen my wife's face, it looked like all the blood drained from her face into my face and onto the floor." Jonathan chuckled. His charming mannerism worked again and he was through to board the international flight to London, England on British Comet Airlines, and then catch the train to Dover, get on the ferry and take the train into Paris. He sat in his first class seat pleased with himself for his escape, but grieved that he would never see his daughter, Nicole again. It had ended so badly. To think that's what he had left in his wake, the consequences of his choices. He had been so wrapped up in his own world of criminal activity that he never noticed what he was doing to his daughter, or what he had become. Wealth had anesthetized him to what was really important in life, love. His greed bred selfishness and extinguished kindness

151

long ago. He was a criminal on the run, a thief, a con, a corrupted soul who actually enjoyed the game of committing a crime and getting away with it. He was an amoral thrill seeker who forfeited it all for a counterfeit life. He closed his eyes and he was over the Atlantic Ocean. Only the broken people were left behind, and he was gone.

# CHAPTER 21

# THE WEDDING ANNOUNCEMENT

*" ...the master of the feast had tasted the water that was made wine."*

*John 2:9 NKJV*

"We're going to turn water into wine, Steven, it looks like this incident can have a happy ending after all. The Reynolds have agreed to our plan and we're making the wedding announcement between Catherine and Jesse today to the press. It's taking place at Monet's photo shoot in Danton Square at 3pm. Ah, the sun is shinning once again, the backdrop for the photo shoot is summer love and the press are going to eat this up. It's the feel good factor that will distract the public from the current issues and put a human face to this election. And who would have thought a Christian's sin would have rejuvenated our campaign." The Governor proclaimed with measured excitement.

Steven , the Chairman of the Democratic Party from Washington D.C. mused over the Governor's words before responding. "I'll believe it when the election is over and you're our next senator, Stan. As per your message, Joshua is writing some press releases for you and will have those to you within the hour. Now remember, you promised to keep Jesses' faith marginalized, we don't want him becoming a spokesperson for you or this campaign."

"Be assured, he will be surrounded by my staff who have already been briefed on how to contain him." The Governor assured Steven. "Oh and, Steven , thank everybody for me for helping my daughter and Jesse gain entrance into Oxford."

"That's what we're her for, Stan, you may not know this but I was a Oxford scholar and have been a guest lecturer from time to time ever since

I've been in office. I was your ace in the hole, as well as supplying the generous donation." Steven related.

"I didn't know that, and I hope the kids do justice to your reputation while they're there. Now I must be running, I have a full schedule today as you can imagine, good-by Steven ." The Governor finished.

While the Governor was making his phone call to Washington, Jesse and his parents were meeting with Pastor Greg to explain the fulfillment of the prophecy by Evangelist Mary Sutton. Pastor Greg sat there mystified by such an interpretation of the prophetic word. "Let me see if I'm hearing you correctly, you believe, Jesse, that God is asking you to be the sacrificial lamb for the Stone family, to endure this injustice in silence so God's grace can bring redemption to them?"

"That's more or less the idea." Jesse confessed.

Pastor Greg appeared frozen as he contemplated this drama. "I heard a sermon years ago by a pastor from New Orleans. While preaching at his Wednesday night service he noticed a teenage girl walk in late and sit near the front. It was summer time which meant it was extremely hot and humid, which is why he noticed her, because she was wearing a long sleeve turtle knit sweater and full length pants. He meant to talk to her after the service but she slipped out before he could reach her.

As he thought about her, he felt she was covering something up with her clothes because they were not the fashion that a young person would normally wear, especially in summertime. If she came back again he made up his mind that he was going to talk with her. And sure enough she came back the following week. When the service was over his ushers began talking with her until the pastor could catch up with her.

He asked her into his office to discover if his suspicious were true. She was demure in character, self-conscious and reserved. Her head was down with her hair covering her face. He told her that he suspected she was a victim of home abuse which is why she covered herself up with her clothes. As he encouraged her to go to the police to put a stop to this abuse, assuring her that as a church they could find her a good home, she started crying. Her tears stopped him from continuing, then she looked up at the pastor and said, "if you take me out of my home, who will tell my mother about Jesus?" He discovered that the girl's mother was a prostitute as well as an alcoholic, thus the abuse. The pastor was astonished at this young girl's grasp of the love of God. As a matter of fact, he was ashamed of his seemingly good intention compared to the girl's purity of heart. He said this young girl preached the greatest sermon he had ever heard. She knew more about divine love at the age of 16 than he did."

"And I'm inclined to believe him. Jesse, you're preaching the same sermon to us, you're willing to suffer and lose your reputation while most of us would want you to save our good name, just the opposite of what Jesus taught. I commend you Jesse, Mary was right, God has chosen the Calvary road for you and I will do everything I can to support you. You have my silence and my prayers on this subject."

Monet, Catherine, the photo crew, the Governor's staff and Jim and Andy were already at Danton Square setting up for the shoot by the time Jesse and his parents arrived. When the Governor and his wife appeared some of the press were milling around inquiring for any pre announcement news they could get.

Actually everybody wanted to met this Jesse. Who was he, where did he come from, what's his family background, why the suddenness of the wedding? The Governor was spinning his version of events, and because of who he was the press couldn't avoid him. His staff were everywhere, intervening, interrupting, interloping, interposing.

Monet was working her magic, and she needed to. Getting Catherine and Jesse to look like the young lovers was paramount. She was fashioning them into positions, molding their facial expression, shouting commands and coaching them like Eleanor Roosevelt . As for Catherine and Jesse, they were thrown into embraces, handholding, fun loving posses, gazing, and the dreaded kisses. Monet like a surgeon was exacting every emotion of love and affection out of the couple for the world to behold. It was a trail by fire for the couple and the press went away eager to print their photos and publish their story in tomorrows news, and fill the news that evening with the 'personal' story of the election.

Romantic love, how it drugs the heart and blinds the eyes, and that was what the Governor was counting on. A public emotionally mesmerized by this young politically connected couple. The Governor was giddy with delight at the mileage he could benefit out of this marriage.

They all dispersed by early evening and the gossipers was churning out the news of the couples upcoming wedding. Pictures taken by by-passers, early releases from various press agents who were there, and of course the spin story by Joshua the speech writer with high quality photo's from Monet, all to give the Governor's slant believability. By mid evening friends, various relatives, students, neighbors, acquaintances and anybody who was somebody knew about the wedding. Senator Jackson and his staff were all talking about it, wondering how they didn't see this coming. Jackson naturally thought the worst, *I wonder if they have to get married? I may have another job for Glenn.*

The following day Ted and his girlfriend were reading the news with interest as well. "I was just with her several weeks ago at one of our college parties." Ted exclaimed to his girlfriend. "She didn't even have a boyfriend then, how can she be getting married so soon. Unless her dad arranged all of this, which I wouldn't put passed him. He's a first class schemer, it's probably just to boost his ratings in the poll, you know, like the wedding between Ingrid Bergman and Roberto Rossellini. . The whole world was caught up in that fairly tale".

"He's dreamy, no wonder she fell for him." His girl blurred out.

"Ha, I'm right her babe, are you saying he's cooler than me?" Ted interrupted with annoyance.

"No, you know you're my sugar Ted, besides, he doesn't have the muscles you have." She voiced with a seductive tone.

"You're connected with her friends, aren't you, through your cousin Ann?" Ted inquired.

"Yeah." She responded

"Give her a call and lets invite her over to see what we can learn about this Jesse and why they're getting married so quickly, I'm just a little suspicious and curious." Ted said thoughtfully.

"Sure, what time tomorrow and where?" She asked.

"It doesn't really matter, whenever she can make it, and let's meet at George's diner ." Ted explained.

Tomorrow just happened to work for Ann, Ted's girlfriends cousin, so at noon they all met at the diner. .

Ted, his girlfriend and Ann were drinking their floats as Ann answered their questions. "They met this summer, had a whirlwind romance and he swept her off her feet. We were all surprised. Catherine went from a power woman to a goofy teenager, like celebrities who met on a movie set and the next thing you know they're married. Ted's girlfriend sat there with her elbows on the table and her face in her hands interjecting with ah's and oh's, and then said, "That's so romantic Ted."

"That's stupid," Ted blared. "The brightest and the most connected had been trying to snag her for years and this dark horse comes out of nowhere and enchants her with his charisma? I don't buy it. Her father groomed her for prominence... position. Who is this Jesse? I've never heard of him, or even seen him."

"I don't know everything because Catherine has been a little preoccupied this summer, but I do know her dad was 100% behind this marriage." Ann said reassuringly to Ted.

"It's got be about the election, the Governor does nothing that doesn't enhance his chances for winning. I must say though, this is a master stroke, like a fake pass in our football games. He has everybody looking at this wedding and not the issues. He is playing a good strategic game."

Ann was concerned when she left Ted and his girlfriend, Ted was visibly dubious, and it sounded like he might make some noise. He had influence and it could bring some suspicion on the wedding. She would need to call Catherine.

* * * * *

"Glenn, I know you just got home from the hospital and you're recuperating from the car accident, but I have another job for you. Do you feel up to it?" Senator Jackson asked.

"As long as it doesn't involved hand to hand combat, I should be OK." Glenn replied.

"Have you seen the news about Governor Stan's daughter, Catherine and her wedding?" Jackson inquired.

"It's all over the news now, you can't miss it, but I'm trying to avoid it." Glenn said sounding cheeky.

"I've got my misgivings about it and I think it may be worth our while to look into it. We need to find out why she's getting married so urgently." Jackson voiced with a skeptical tone.

"I see what you're getting at, leave it to me. I still have a few friends on campus and I'll put my ear to the ground and see what is on the rumor mill." Glenn replied.

"And if you do come up with something, there will be an extra bonus in it for you, we only have a few months left until the election and this wedding is going to increase his poll rating, we need something soon and it needs to be a monstrous scandalous." Jackson ended.

Several minutes later Glenn turned off his video game again as a call came in from Jackson's assistant, "Glenn, Jackson wanted me to ask you to investigate the boys she may have been dating over the past couple of months, as well as any parties Catherine went too, you know what goes on at those college parties. If she's pregnant then she can't be more than a few months." The assistant stated.

"I'm on it, only I'm going to need a car until the insurance settles the claim on my Corvette." Glenn asked.

"Use your American Express credit card and rent something, we'll take care of the expense when it's due." The assistant replied.

Danton University was on summer break but all the calendar events and house parties were in their past college papers. It didn't take Glenn long to find the pictures and the parties Catherine had gone to. Everybody took pictures of her and gave them to the papers, , she was a college celebrity for most kids. And there it was, Ted and Catherine throwing down shots at the final party of the year, and they were looking real close. As he explored the various papers relating to Danton University he began to put a thread together of rumors, pictures, denial statements, conquests and students boasting. And Ted the tight-end of the football team was A-listed for his sexual conquests, which included Catherine. Could it be that obvious? It was the best lead he had and his next step was to find Ted and befriend him in someway.

Ted's information was in all of the papers because he was a popular football star. Glenn drove over to Ted's house and began following him. He discovered Ted didn't have to work because his mom was the head administrator of Danton Hospital and his father was a CEO of an electronics company. Money was not an issue for him. He went from Drive in's to shops, , from sports centers to friends' houses, from street racing to *bashes . He was a never ending pleasure-seeker. Glenn could see that he was a Casanova in the making, a person to be avoided.

Glenn made his move, he entered George's diner and found the table next to the one Ted and his girl usually sat at. He had the invitation to Catherine and Jesses wedding, courtesy of Jackson who had received several out of political politeness . Jackson said that the Governor knew he would be dubiously inquisitive and that an invitation was a ploy to deflect his skepticism.

Ted and his girl came in and had their usual drinks, chatting about their meaningless *round up time. . Glenn stood up, turned around and stumbled into Ted's table dropping the wedding invitation onto their table. Ted shouted, "watch it man, my girl is here."

"I'm sorry, I just had a car accident and I'm weaker than I thought I was." Glenn spoke pathetically.

Ted could see from Glenn's face some bruises and cuts that were mending and apologized for his rudeness. As Ted reached for the invitation to give back to Glenn he noticed it was the same wedding invitation his parents received.

"You're going to Catherine's wedding?" Ted asked.

"Yes, but I must say, it does seem a bit abrupt, her getting married so quickly." Glenn implied suspicion.

"You can say that again, I've known Catherine a long time and this wedding doesn't fit her profile." Ted insisted.

"I would agree with you, I wonder if she's pregnant?" Glenn put the elephant in the room to be examined and see how he would respond.

"That's exactly what I was thinking, what's your name anyway?" Ted said suddenly realizing he didn't know this person he was talking to.

"Bill," Glenn never gave out his real name when investigating, "I think she may have gotten pregnant at one of those college parties." Glenn was dancing close to the edge now but he didn't have time to pirouette around this possibility because Jackson needed something now to reverse the polling rating. The Governor had gained 3 points in the polls since the wedding was announced. Ted went red in the face, his eyes had a look of sudden terror realizing he and Catherine *made out together at their last college party. The pieces of his misgivings about this wedding aligned with foreboding.

"Are you alright Ted," his girlfriend's voice punctuated the momentary silence Glenn's last words had caused.

"Ted, can I talk to you alone?" Glenn asserted into Ted's bewilderment.

"I guess so, wait here Angie while we go outside for a minute." Ted instructed his girlfriend.

Glenn and Ted walked outside the cafe and found a spot to be alone. "Listen Ted, I'm sorry to spring this on you so suddenly, but my meeting you today is no accident, I had a hunch that you may have been the one who got Catherine pregnant, and from the look on your face in there, it seems I maybe right." Glenn spoke frankly.

"I don't know who you are and what you may think you know but I'm not confessing anything to a stranger." Ted shot back at him.

"Ted, I'm a journalist, and I'm going to write the story with or without you, but I would rather get all my facts right and give you the profit of being my source." Glenn had been well schooled by Jackson's people on how to pry information out of people and it was paying off with Ted.

Ted was seething, he felt he had fumbled the ball and the only way he knew how to handle this type of maneuver was become more aggressive. Push back, knock your opponent down and run through him. But he was not on the football field, this was real life played with different rules.

Glenn interrupted his flare up, "our paper will pay you big money for a story like this, and I guarantee we will keep your name out of it." Glenn was pushing hard because he felt this was his only opportunity and if he let Ted slip out of this he would lose him, so he kept the pressure on.

"How much money are we talking about here, Bill?" Ted asked jittery.

"At least $20,000." Glenn assured him with a patronizing look.

"Ok, I had sex with her a couple of months ago but there's no way for me to know if she became pregnant, besides, if she was knocked up, she would be the type of girl to have an abortion." Ted intimated. They talked for about 20 minutes as Glenn was recording his story on his reel to reel in his briefcase as he had with the Governor, , and then they parted company. Glenn immediately called Jackson's assistant to give him the good news and tomorrow they would work out the next step of their strategy. This was too good to be true.

# CHAPTER 22

# THE TWO SCHEMES

*"The man of integrity walks securely, but he who takes crooked paths will be found out."*

*Proverbs. 10:9 NIV*

Nicole was released from the hospital along with a long list of aftercare instructions. She couldn't drive home, was to get plenty of rest, keep her environment quiet, take Aspirin for any headaches, no drinking of alcohol and eat small amounts of food for a few days. She was even thinner than before but her first concern was her mom. Nicole knew her mom was the fragile one in the family. And her dad, was the detective right or was he just trying to scare her into saying something that would incriminate him. Not that it mattered, she would love to see him suffer for all the torment he put the family through. And then there was Jesse, what had become of him? And for herself, unhinged, that was the word that best described her world.

Nicole's mom related the whole sordid affair with her dad, the accusations and the fact that Jonathan was now officially a fugitive of law as they drove home. He had vanished without a trace. Coco sobbed intermittently as she choked the story out. When they pulled into their driveway her mom stopped the car and said, "I don't think your dad is coming back, he has deserted us being the coward he is." Then she wept uncontrollably. Nicole could tell she was back on meds but she was elated that her dad may never be back again.

"I'm ecstatic that he's gone mom, and I hope the police hunt him down and throw him into prison for good." Nicole articulated as an expression of liberation.

"Well, at least he left us some money, he always was a good provider." It was one of the last things Jonathan did while he sat at his desk before leaving. He wrote Coco and Nicole a letter with a safe deposit key, which is where Coco had found the money.

* * * * *

On the other side of the world Jonathan had made his way to France where, for cash many years ago, he had purchased a cottage in an idyllic village outside of Paris. He knew that most of his contacts or houses were either being watched or were compromised, so he decided to lay low while on the lam from the police. He had enough money to last for several years and he would just enjoy his time until he could come up with another scheme. Even though France had an extradition treaty with the US Jonathan still felt safe there because his property was purchased under a false identity before he even became involved in dealing with diamonds. It was all part of his long term planning that had now fallen apart not because of his business dealings, but because he failed to love his family. Greed had replaced his own flesh and blood and had become his lover. For the first time he had some space in his life to feel the emptiness of his choices. He was going to need some more wine.

Nicole was not the only one to come home, the conspirator Glenn had also come back to plague the Governor. "We've been keeping tabs on Glenn and we're sad to say, he's got the scent of Catherine's pregnancy, and he's going to be sharing his suppositions with Jackson tomorrow." Andy told the Governor.

"I should have buried him when I had the opportunity years ago, I never thought he would have come back to haunt me." The Governor brooded.

"This is a potential disaster and calls for extreme measures, but we have a course of action planned and simply need you to give us the green light, you don't need to know the details but we're not going to act unilaterally here, we're not going to move without your permission." Jim stated.

"I want you to put the fear of God into him this time, it's time to remove this pebble from my shoe and get Senator Jackson off of my back." The Governor confirmed.

"Say no more." Andy replied, consider it done.

Andy and Jim knew that Glenn was meeting with Jackson at 4pm that day because of the bugs they had planted in his house. Their surveillance had paid off again and they were glad his employees had the foresight to keep a watch on Glenn. They arrived at Glenn's apartment and rang his doorbell. Glenn took forever to answer because he was so absorbed in his gaming. Glenn opened the door hesitantly and poked his head out to see the two men standing there.

"Are you Glenn Watson?" Andy inquired

"Yes, what do you want and who are you?" Glenn asked distrustfully.

Andy and Jim showed Glenn their FBI badges and said, "we're from the FBI and we would like to ask you a few questions about Senator Jackson and your involvement with him. We would like you to come with us because we have some further questions for you as well."

"Just a minute while I get my shoes on." Glenn said nervously.

"Leave the door open, we don't want you running off now, do we?" Jim said brassily. He was enjoying this.

They got into the car and Andy drove them to an empty warehouse on the outside of Danton near Westfield. Andy stopped the car abruptly, they jumped out and opened the door for Glenn, grabbed his arms and walked him inside while he protested and mentioned that he was just in a car accident and was fragile. It was a large cavernous space inside the old industrial building with scraps of metal, forgotten office furniture and out dated machinery scattered about. At the end was a lone cold metal chair that they sat Glenn down in and tied his hands behind the back of the chair, but loosely.

"Now what is it the boss told us to do with him? " Jim asked flippantly.

"Make the problem go away," said Andy as he gestured with his Smith and Wesson 44 magnum in his hand.

Glenn's eyes widened and he shuddered out, "what do you guys want, you're not the FBI are you?"

"You see Mr. Black, we have a smart one here," Jim snidely remarked and then turned on Glenn. He leaned into his face and shouted like a drill sergeant, "we're the ones with the badges, we're the ones with the guns and we're the ones asking the questions, now, tell us, about the millions of dollars your employer overcharged the state government years ago. And what about the money you embezzled from the Mayor and the city of Danton?"

"So you see we are FBI, and we know everything," Andy punctuated with a stern face. "And where is all that money coming from that has been deposited into your account over the past 8 years, and where will you get the $20,000 to give to Ted for his story?" Glenn's face went ashen. "Oh yes, you're in a lot of trouble with the IRS for tax evasion, just think of the back taxes. And the fraud department, they want a piece of you as well. And we want you for bribery, embezzlement, defrauding the federal government, extortion and public corruption of governmental personnel. Shall I go on Mr. Watson or are you going to cooperate with us and start giving us names!"

Glenn had been working the rope lose behind his chair and he was free now. His body was aching from his car accident but panic was gripping him and he knew he had to get out of there or he was facing real prison time, to say nothing of what it would do to Senator Jackson. Jim suddenly announced, "all this excitement has gone to my blabber, I've got to go Andy, now just you wait here Mr. Watson until I get back." And then he thumped Glenn on the forehead.

After Jim left the room Andy took a step towards Glenn and pretended to stumble and fall, head banging Glenn and tumbling down. He shot his gun into the air to scare Glenn into fleeing, and it worked. Glenn jumped up kicking over the chair and started running for all his life at the door behind him. Andy shouted out, "Stop, stop or I'll shot," but Glenn was charging like a bull for his escape. Andy let off another shot into the ceiling and Glenn was out the door scampering like a frightened dog.

Jim returned with a smile on his face saying, "I think we handled that *swell, don't you Andy?"

"Like clock work, he may never stop running now. We're keeping tabs on him to make sure he doesn't divulge his story and is completely gone this time. Andy and Jim did not have to worry. Glenn galloped until he was out of breath, caught a cab to his house, threw some cloths and games into his suitcase and spilt out of Danton heading for his condo in Florida. He called Jackson's assistant and told them he had been apprehended by the FBI and how they knew everything he had done and was doing. He told them they had hacked his computer and phone and were even aware of the $20,000 he was going to give to Ted. He was talking so fast he was breathless. His stomach was in knots and his head pounding. He was having an adrenaline rush, ran out of his apartment, jumped into his car and couldn't drive fast enough. Glenn wouldn't deluge more detail to Jackson for fear it would further incriminate him, he was out for good now.

Andy and Jim were happy to report to the Governor and to Steven that the problem was taken care of and their secret was safe, for now anyway. The political machinery had worked it's magic and Democratic schemers could all lived to fight another day.

While Andy and Jim were scaring the life out of Glenn, Catherine was hatching her plan to unmask her stalker. She had arranged for her whole leadership fraternal to be waiting in the spill over parking lot of the Westfield shopping centre, and they were there with the necessary arsenal. She knew that the Chrysler would follow her so Catherine led the woman into her trap. As Catherine pulled into the parking lot Olivia followed her, staying about a quarter of mile behind. Catherine had about 25 girls there who looked like they were practicing cheerleading moves. But as Olivia's Chrysler was passing the girls driving slowly, they started walking across the front of her car. Hannah then hit the Chrysler with her megaphone falling down simultaneously making it look like she was hit by the car.

Olivia stomped on the breaks, jumped out of the car and ran to Hannah thinking she had hit her. Hannah lay there holding her leg, moaning and contorting her face. As soon as Olivia knelt down to help Hannah, all the other girls grabbed Olivia, her arms and legs, her head and thighs, her torso and hair. Several girls were sitting on her before Olivia could figure out what was going on. She was taken completely by surprise, whoever would have expected college girls to attack a special agent. The girls went to work with precision and utter determination. They held her feet and legs together and started wrapping her in duck tap working their way up to her waist and on to her shoulders. They then put some tape over her mouth and put a bag over her eyes, then threw her into Catherine's trunk.

"Thank you girls, you were awesome. I will let you know what happens." They all said their good-bye's and Catherine drove back to her house with Beth, Ann and Hannah. When they got there Catherine drove into her garage and closed the automatic garage door. They opened her trunk, lifted Olivia out and hung her upside down from the metal trusses running across the garage ceiling. Olivia was struggling, wiggling, screaming in muffled tones and livid with anger. They took the bag of her eyes and started the interrogation.

"Now we'd like to take the tape off of your mouth but if you're going to scream or rant and go all ape on us , then we'll leave it on and just walk out of this garage and leave you hanging upside until you are willing to answer a few of my questions." Catherine said authoritatively. "So, can I assume you're willing to cooperate, or are you going to be immature about all of this, after all, you're the one who's been stalking me. If you're willing to answer, just blink twice."

As Catherine watched Olivia blink twice she felt her old self again, assertive, in control, she was writing her own biography once more and it felt good. "I want to know who you are and why you have been following me these past weeks." Catherine ripped the tape off of her mouth and Olivia gasped in pain.

"Before I tell you, can we talk in private, this information is for you and you alone." Olivia panted out.

"No, I want everybody to hear this, they're my witnesses and this is the cost of you getting caught, which I'm sure is very embarrassing for you, a professional I assume." Catherine replied condescendingly with a look of self-importance.

"Ok, but it's your responsibility and you'll have to explain to your father." Olivia answered.

"I knew my father had to be behind this in some way, so who are you and why are you following me?" Catherine retorted back.

"My name is Olivia and I work for a special branch of security out of Washington, and we have been sent to watch over you and your dad just until the election. In case any problems should arise."

"Your secret service?" Catherine came back wide eyed.

"No, they only protect the president and his family, and a few other people. We're from a department nobody knows about, freelance you might say." Olivia answered. "Now, can you let me down and unwrap me before I have a brain hemorrhage?"

They let her down, painstakingly removed all the duck tape and looked at each other as though they were in trouble. "I think maybe we should go Catherine," Hannah said, "and let the two of you figure out what you want to do next."

"That's a good idea girls," Olivia said.

The three girls walked out and were giggling as they went, proud of themselves for bagging such a catch as her, and as they reached the side door Hannah yelled out, "it's always an adventure being with you Cath."

"Thank you my partners in crime, we cracked the case." Catherine yelled back jokingly.

Catherine and Olivia talked for over an hour covering the last several weeks of her father's alliance with Washington D.C. and why all the protection was needed with him running for presidency in 8 years. Olivia apologized for being so obvious and that they may take her off the job now because of her failure. But Catherine told her she wouldn't say anything, now that she knew, she didn't want to start all over again with someone she didn't know.

\* \* \* \* \*

It was a hectic day for Danton, Nicole returning home to a fatherless family, Glenn hightailing it to Florida thinking he was running from the law. Senator Jackson's potential smear campaign vanishing up in smoke and the mystery woman unmasked.

Catherine drove Olivia back to her car and returned home pleased with herself until she remembered the leadership dance she had to go to, and she would have to go with Jesse, who knew nothing about it as of yet. A melancholy thought intruded on her happiness of today, because today was a distillation of all that she loved and cherished - sovereign over her destiny. Today she made her own karma and not her father, nor the baby, nor politics.

# CHAPTER 23

# THE DANCE

*"a time to weep and a time to laugh, a time to mourn and a time to dance..."*

*Ecclesiastes 3:4 NIV*

Jesse was reading the newspaper before he set off for work, dreading the reporters outside his house. 'Liberal marries Conservative,' 'Atheist weds Born-again Believer,' 'The Election Wedding,' 'Dark Horse Wins Her Hand,' the headlines read. And right across the page was a half page add for Hula Hoops. How fitting, all is fun and games. The Governor's strategy had worked, his ratings were soaring and the potential scandal suppressed. But the papers were having a field day with the Governor caricatures of him. The papers were demonstrating vivid imagination. The Danton Chronicle ran a cartoon of the Governor holding a pitch fork with a halo, while the Danton press showed him as a preaching politician with a bible in his hands. The Telegraph's satirical depiction was of a double profile shot, the left side of the face was Eisenhower on the right side and on the left John F. Kennedy.

Senator Jackson had been defeated in his last two attempts to smear Stan and was beginning to lose his way in the campaign. His political imperatives were being diminished by the media storm over the wedding. It had captured the imagination of the whole state. Already t-shirt's, mugs and a whole range of trinkets were selling off the shelves. Journalists were following Jesse and Catherine all over town, even camping outside their houses. In a last ditch effort Jackson was trying to revive his black roots historical connection with John Marrant, the first American black preacher, who addressed the, 'equality of all men before God,' in 1789. History was important to this part of the country but his voice was being drowned out with the hip and trivial.

He was quoting Job to his staff as he watched the polls rising in favor of Stan, "The thing I feared has come upon me."

As soon as Jesse pushed his front door open the questions began to flow. "Why do you think Catherine chose you over every other guy, Jesse?" One journalist asked.

"Because I love her," was Jesse's simple answer, (though not in a romantic sense), trying to avoid too obtrusive questions. Another journalist shoved a mic into his face and blurted out, "Why the rush to get married, is there something we should all know about Jesse?"

Jesse stopped and looked at all the reporters, motioned with his hands for quiet and calm, then began, "There are a number of reasons for the quickness of the wedding, first of all, I didn't want her to change her mind." And they all laughed. "Then suddenly we both found ourselves going to England for university in September, so getting married now just made more sense. And, her father the Governor thought this would be good for his election." Again all the reporters laughed and started making comments like, "You got that right Jesse," and "It seems to be working," and "We underestimated how clever he was." Then the big question came from a female reporter from channel 5, "So how did the two of you meet?"

"We actually met 5 years ago and have both gone to the same high school and now Danton University together." Jesse successfully defected the question.

"And how did you pop the big question?" Another reporter asked excitedly.

"You're not going to believe this, but you already know I believe in miracles," and they all chuckled again, "it was in her father's study, right in front of him." And that created a commotion among all the reporters. They couldn't decide if he was a saint or unimaginative, a gentleman in a day of forgotten manners or a puppet of the Governor.

"Now I really do have to get to work, so please excuse me." And Jesse was off. His interview was aired at noon and Stan, his campaign party and the people in Washington D.C. were all impressed with his answers and mannerism. Jesse on the other hand was finding these press interviews conflicting. Not exposing Catherine and her family while being truthful was a delicate balancing act.

As Jesse was entering the cycling shop the phone rang and the owner said it was for him. , "Hello Catherine, this is a nice surprise." Jesse answered.

"Why do you insist on being so swell, are all Christians spineless?" Catherine spoke before she thought, and immediately regretted what she had said since she was calling for a favor. "I'm sorry Jesse, let's rewind, how are you today?"

"Conflicted." Jesse replied.

"Conflicted, what does that mean, who tells anybody what they're really feeling when you ask them how they are? You're so arcane, I don't get you at all Jesse."

Jesse decided to move the conversation on and said, "is there something you wanted Catherine, I have to start work?"

"Yes, sorry, there's a dance tonight for our leadership fraternal, which is for all the fraternity and sorority community, and I just realized, you need to be my date, you're my fiancé now. And Monet is going to be there again using it as a photo op for my father's campaign. And since we're being followed I'm sure the press will be there masquerading as students. It slipped everybody's mind which is why I'm calling you at such a late date." Catherine queried.

"I would love to, is this formal and what time should I pick you up? Jesse asked.

"If you pick me up at 8 it will mean the place will be full before we get there, we need to be fashionably late and then we can better avoid the reporters." Catherine purposed. "And yes Jesse, it is formal."

"I'll be there." And Jesse started work.

On the way home Jesse stopped off at Mr. Smart, a tuxedo store to pick up his order. He had gone over there during his lunch hour and fortunately they were able to do all the alterations in record time. That's because Jesse had become somewhat of a celebrity around town, and when he walked into their shop, they were going to move heaven and earth to meet his needs. The soon to be son-in-law of the Governor and possibly the next senator. This was an achievement for them.

At 8:15 pm Jesse rang the doorbell of the Stone's mansion, at least that's how he saw their house. This time he was greeted not by the maid, but by a *decked out, *knocked out Catherine. Dressed in her Channel evening gown with her hair pulled back into a beautiful knot placed at the top of the head, Jesse was staring at elegancy and grace. She looked like a goddess, he thought. Almost a full five seconds passed before Catherine realized that she had been staring at Jesse. When she caught herself, she blushed and said, "Um, ready?" Jesse smiled. "I am. You look really gorgeous, by the way, Miss Stone." He offered her his arm but she didn't take it, and he pretended not to notice.

Olivia was parked down the road with her new Ford and kept her distance now, she was so grateful to Catherine for not disclosing her complete failure as an agent to her dad.

Catherine snuck a glance at Jesse again as they walked to the car. In his tuxedo he looked stunning. She had trouble concealing her pleasant surprise. Despite this, however, she refused to treat him like a friend. He's still the moron who got her into this mess, she thought. "I'm only going with you tonight because I have to," she said.

"I know." Jesse said as he opened the car door for her.

"Ah, no, I don't think we're going in this car, what is this by the way?" Catherine asked.

"It's a Rambler ." Jesse responded more as an apology then an answer.

"We have to keep up appearances, remember, I am the Governor's daughter, and if the press sees us drive up in this 'thing' it will be the next front page spread of our ongoing humiliation. Let's take my Thunderbird, it's what they'll be expecting." Catherine smiled as they moved over to her car, she loved being in control.

"You know, you're such a pushover." Catherine sermonized.

"I see it more as being understanding." Jesse said.

"And I'm only letting you drive because of expectations, you do know how to drive a high performance car? " Catherine said sarcastically.

"I'm more versatile then you think." Jesse remarked with a smile.

"And, look at this Mr. Understanding " as she was pointing to her stomach. "I'm showing. This is beyond embarrassing. I'm getting fat because of all you men." Catherine complained.

"All us men?" Jesse repeated.

"Yeah, You, my dad, Ted." Catherine mentioned.

"Ted?" Jesse said with surprise.

"Oh! Uh, I mean, yeah, Ted. That's what I've decided to name the baby if it's a boy." Her cheeks flushed bright red.

Jesse knew the truth, but he only laughed at her gently, he started the car and they drove off. Jesse knew of Ted. Ted was one of those rich, arrogant guys who needed to prove his manhood. Jesse was suddenly angry and realized it was not going to be easy to forgive. He liked it better not knowing who the father was.

"Hey, we're here," Jesse said, "I'll drop you off and go park the car."

As she started to get out of the car she turned back and said, "You know this is my last chance to have fun and be me. That means I will be dancing with other guys as well."

"After you see me dance, you'll know what a smart move that is." Jesse said.

"Urrr, you *burn me up, " she said with a scowl. "You're doing it again." Catherine said reproachfully.

"What?" Jesse asked.

"You're being *kookie , a pushover. " As Catherine was saying these words she felt a small pang of disappointment. Amazed, she realized that she wanted him to be jealous.

"You mean understanding," Jesse said in a matter-of -fact way.

"Whatever, so, let me ask you something. How many girls have you gone out with these past four years?" Catherine looked at him pensively.

"Counting you?" Jesse asked.

"Yes."

"One." Jesse already knew the look she was going to give him. He had seen it many times throughout high school and at University when students found out he was a Christian through their conversations.

"I knew it." Catherine said looking smug. "So, if you've never been with a girl, how do you know you love me?"

"Because I'm willing to forfeit my future to protect you from the consequences of...of your situation." Jesse retorted.

Catherine was rarely without a reply, but this dumbfounded her. But just at that moment, one of the hosts opened the door and said to them, "Welcome to the party!"

As she walked up the stairs she felt ashamed for the first time in her life. An emotion she was not accustomed to. She was always in the dominant roll, holding the leverage over other people. When she got to the hall and stood there looking around Jesse appeared at her side quicker than she anticipated. "Ready?" Jesse asked. She squared her shoulders and said, "I can do this. Let's party!" She threw a smile at him and they went in.

Monet was waiting as they entered, and she began snapping away. Flashes were going off, and other photographers were scurrying around them. The crowd soon became aware of their presence and all eyes went on them as they strolled down the carpeted pathway. Monet was shouting instructions, friends and college students yelled out for attention, every camera and reporter dressed in formal attire were shoving mic's into the couples face simultaneously machine gunning questions.

Although she didn't expect it, the evening was an cool night for Catherine. The popular guys all wanted to dance with her and her friends made her feel like her old self. She felt young, beautiful and without a care. The only negative part of the evening for her was how she kept noticing for

175

the first time how all the guys kept making stupid jokes or trying to touch her while they were dancing. She had never thought before how annoying they were. She was almost relieved when Jesse cut in while she was dancing with one of the guys. But she was also surprised by her reaction when every girl in the place wanted to dance with Jesse. She had never been possessive, and this person of no consequence was swiftly emerging into the limelight

By the end of the evening as the slow songs were being played, Catherine and Jesse were actually touching each other as they danced. He held her around her waist and she held him close around his neck. They weren't saying anything, only looking into each others' eyes. Being so close, Jesse could see her eyes clearly. .

"Your eyes really are emerald," he remarked.

"Yeah." Catherine reacted.

"I always thought you wore *corneals." Jesse suggested.

"Is that what you thought when you were stalking me?" Catherine said with a sheepish smile.

"They're beautiful." Jesse said with tenderness.

Catherine was flustered and was blushing for the second time. "Thank you," she muttered.

It was their first conversation without the usual coldness or unkind banter, she was relaxing her resolve of never capitulating to his kindness. Everybody around them was staring at them because they looked like a couple who only had eyes for each other. Beth, Ann and Hannah were taken back by the amour that seemed to be haloing over them. This was not their Catherine, it appeared to them that Jesse was having a definite influence on her.

It turned into a moment as Jesse and Catherine seemed to be unaware that the crowd had become spectators, all cameras were on them and a spontaneous clamor rose up in a unanimous voice, "kiss, kiss, kiss, kiss, kiss, kiss......" the shout went on until Jesse and Catherine realized they were appealing to them. They turned their faces to the crowd and went red with embarrassment. They knew at that moment they had to satisfy the public's demands, and so they turned their eyes back toward each other slowly tilting their heads in opposite directions drawing closer to each other's lips, both tentatively, Catherine not wanting to appear compliant and Jesse not desiring to take advantage. They gradually, cautiously, anxiously and ever so gingerly moved to kiss while the noise of the crowd increased, and then their lips touched, pressed, sealed. Jesse's right hand was embracing the back of Catherine's neck while his other hand was around the small of her back. Catherine's arms were wrapped around Jesse's body and Hannah gave an audible gasp. Her response set off a chain reaction and the whole crowd ahhh'd.

It was Jesse's first real kiss, his heart pounding, feeling breathless and sensing the softness of her pulsating lips. Catherine was startled, his kiss was gentle with intensity, igniting adoring desires that was sweeping her off her feet. It was not a kiss of wanting but one of giving. They lingered as their lips captured each other. The crowd was watching adagio music being composed through their kissing. Then Jesse's lips unhurriedly parted from Catherine's and the place erupted with cheers and applause, cameras flashing and the volume of the music coming up. Judy Garland's words came to Catherine's mind, words she had heard Beth, the film buff, quote many times, "For it was not into my ear you whispered, but into my heart. It was not my lips you kissed, but my soul."

As they left for the evening, Jesse walked Catherine out with his arm around the small of her back, and she liked it. When the porter opened Catherine's door Jesse slipped his hand from behind her back and took her hand to help Catherine into her car. Once in her seat she glanced back at Jesse to catch his eyes and they smiled simultaneously. As Jesse made his way around the car to the driving seat Catherine thought to herself, *what is happening to me, I have never felt these feelings before? It's not excitement, it's not desire, it's more like a comforting serenity. I feel......appreciated, respected.....loved?*

Jesse interrupted her thoughts when he started up the car and began to drive home. Both of them didn't say much but just savored the moment. At Catherine's house Jesse walked Catherine up to her door with the big question shouting through both of their minds, would they kiss? Jesse took Catherine's hand as they walked up her steps. They stopped at the landing in front of the grand doors and faced each other.

Catherine was shocked at how much she wanted Jesse to kiss her, and Jesse was all butterflies at the thought of Catherine's lips touching his. They starred at each other with their eyes revealing the yearning of their hearts. Was it fate, was it chemistry, or was it the gravitation of love that pulled them, slowly, hesitantly, irresistibly together until their lips touched for that summer's night kiss. Their hearts were racing, emotions swelling, and their souls being pierced with longing. A half hope became just perceivable to Catherine, and it raised a thought, *is this what real love feels like?*

Jesse leaned back and with a smile said, "thanks for tonight, I have never enjoyed being a fiancée so much as I have tonight."

"And I had a fab time as well. You're right, there is more to you than meets the eye." Catherine commented with a coy smile.

"Well, good night, and do you want to exchange cars, after all, you have never driven a Rambler ?" Jesse asked with sheepish look as he began to walk away.

"You wish..." Catherine remarked. And with that Jesse was in his car and driving away.

# CHAPTER 24

# THE SHOPPING CENTER

*"For I desire mercy, not sacrifice..."*

*Hosea 6:6 NIV*

The air was thinning out for Jesse, Catherine and the Governor. Ted was taking anti anxiety pills for his newly developed nervous condition, caused by living in fear that he and his family's reputation could be ruined by a leaked story. He regretted taking the money from Glenn as soon as he deposited it, and was relieved when Glenn called him and told him he was not going to run the story. But the uncertainty of it all still haunted him. Glenn was avoiding the Daytona beaches in Florida while searching for some new partners for his next con through his video games, , and living off of the weekly hush money from Jackson. And Jackson was being marginalized more and more in the political race.

It was a good thing because the month of August was incredibly busy for the engaged couple and the Governor– the approaching wedding, campaign appearances, press interviews, planning to move overseas and saying goodbye to friends. With only two weeks left till the wedding, everyday was a new revelation of what needed to be done, passports, turning over obligations, selling their cars and practicing British English verses American English. For most people, it was the little things that seem to mean the most. For Jesse it was no longer making his weekly runs to help his gran, biking with his friends down death drop, playing drums in the worship band at church, and Nick, his high school buddy. His parent's would be tough to leave, they were a tight knit family and he considered his parents his best friends. For Catherine, it was her friends, especially Hannah, the coffee with the girls, plotting covert schemes, being in the limelight with her dad and shopping with her mom.

The Reynolds's and the Stone's were spending more and more time together because of the wedding plans. The Governor kept everybody on task and focused. His wife, Ann Marie, was the "detail lady", writing everything down, making calls and organizing the couples lives. She had hired a wedding coordinator who was making it all happen. The venue, the florist, the reception banquet, the food and ice sculptures, the photographer, music, invites, seating arrangements, limousines, and coordinating the honored guests; Senators, congressmen, press, local politicians from the executive, judicial and legislative departments, the police commissioner and a whole host from Washington D.C. The Governor intended to impress the reporters and let them see who the golden boy was.

The Governor was brilliant at maintaining the image of the happy father-in-law. Jesse's parents were accommodating, and were even warming up to Catherine's family over the weeks. But Catherine remained in denial, reluctantly helping with the wedding plans.

The kiss seemed to thaw Catherine's icy armor, she couldn't believe how genteel Jesse was being. She had never met anyone like him, in the sense that he never wanted anything from her. And that made her uncomfortable. She was boss at keeping guys on a leash, the more they wanted from her the more leverage it gave her to command control. It was a lesson she had learned well from her daddy. With all the other guys, she had always felt like the prey. Yet with Jesse, he actually made her feel like the prize, special. She didn't know if this was an act, and at any moment he would stop being 'the *kookie guy,' and turn out to be like all the other takers. Because she didn't fully trust or understand him, and because she was being forced into something she didn't want to do she was polite but remained reservedly icy and unresponsive to his kindness, even though this was now being mixed with growing ambiguity towards Jesse.

The remaining time before the wedding was madness. The Governor was his own political machine when it came to this wedding. He was running interference with the wedding coordinator, usurping as the PR man, micromanaging the seating and general semblance of the wedding. And nobody was going to tell him how to deal with this matter.

Meanwhile, as the finishing touches were being put on the wedding plans, Mrs. Stone suggested that Catherine and Jesse go to the shopping center to get the last few purchases for the reception. Catherine's frosty attitude was continuing to thaw towards Jesse as the days went on, and she found herself......liking him. Catherine thought shopping was her domain and it could be fun to see how Jesse reacted. His kindness and understanding that had once made her so uncomfortable was now attractive to her. She had never dated anyone like him.

They had a blast at the shopping center , running around, choosing things for their wedding reception, except for the occasional reporter or paparazzi snatching pictures of them.

Catherine liked how Jesse didn't comment on every girl who walked by them, like her old boyfriends used to do. After awhile, Jesse said, "Hey, Catherine."

"Yes?" She said. They were sitting by the center's fountain, taking a much- needed break. .

"Do you mind if we stop by Sakes Fifth Avenue? My best friend Nick works there."

"Sure, I can look at their new autumn line of clothes, they just arrived." Then it hit Catherine, she was making everything about her again. On the way to the store, Catherine said, "So, do you like shopping, because I have to buy a whole new wardrobe every season."

"I like it, but I only buy more clothes when I wear my old one's out." Jesse mentioned. When they got to the store, Catherine couldn't help herself - she headed straight for the newest and most expensive clothes. Jesse walked over to Nick, who was folding at a rack.

"Whoa, this is crazy. I haven't seen you guys actually together outside of press interviews yet," he said. "I saw the photos, but in real life it's surreal, man. You finally got your dream girl." Nick commented.

"I wouldn't say I have her," Jesse replied.

Nick watched her rushing to the rack of clothes. "She's gonna be an expensive one," Nick remarked.

Jesse smiled "I'm trying not to think about it."

"I know you've already explained to me why you are going through with this madness, but she's out of Vogue magazine and you are... are...." Nick stammered

"And what are you trying to say?..." Jesse responded.

"She has way bigger things to do than be a mom at 19." Nick said with his usual insightfulness.

"Yeah, our worlds keep colliding." Remarked Jesse.

"Does she like you?" Nick asked.

"I don't think so," Jesse answered. "She's too hard to read. I'm trying though."

"So tell me again why you're doing this, since she's out to ruin your life? " Nick asked.

"I can tell you Nick because I know you'll understand, at least I hope so, but when the world was pounding the nails into Jesus' hands and feet, he was saying, 'Father, forgive them, for they know not what they do.' Now how can I do any less? I'm just trying to love her the way God love's me." Jesse answered reservedly.

"When did you become so deep, you make me feel like I'm not even a Christian." Nick said contemplatively.

"I don't know if it's deep, maybe just stupid." And they both cracked up.

"Hey, Jesse," Catherine interrupted them, "What do you think?" They both turned. She stood before them in an aqua blue sleeveless summer dress. Just standing there with the price tag still dangling from the dress, she looked like an elegant supermodel. "Well? " she said, but the expression on their faces said everything.

"You look .........perfect!" Jesse managed to say whilst thinking, *is this girl really going to be my wife?*

"You like it then?" Cather said mischievously.

"What's not to like?" Jesse and Nick said in unison.

Catherine walked over to Jesse, grabbed his hand and said, "Feel the fabric, it's chiffon. Have you ever felt it before?"

"Ah no," He ran his hand over the material.

When she bounced back into the dressing room, Nick said, "Maybe God does love you more than me. I should think about suffering more for God, maybe I'll get a goddess as well."

She ended up buying the dress, along with several other things. "I think we'll be visiting Nick here quite often!" She joked. Since she had had such a good response at Sakes, she decided to make an evening of it and visit Macy's and Filene's as well. Many shopping bags later, Jesse asked, "Do you really need all these clothes?"

"No." She laughed

"So why do you buy them?" Jesse asked not understanding the female mind.

"Because I'm worth it," Catherine said as a true drama queen, "You're going to need to know that about me."

"Okay, okay, I agree with that." Jesse acquiesced.

*Is he for real?* She thought. *He really thinks I'm worth it?* She felt her cheeks redden - again.

They ended up at Socrates coffee house, and Nicole was already enjoying her Iced coffee. "Nicole," Catherine said with delight, "you've recovered."

"Hi Cath, it's been awhile....and this is Jesse I assume, your fiancé." Nicole asked.

"Yes, this is Jesse, the one we talked about. How have you been, we have all missed you. So much has happened not only to you but to all of us that it seems ages ago we got together." Catherine was wanting to move the conversation on.

"I've heard a lot about you Jesse, congratulations on the upcoming wedding." Nicole feebly said.

"Thanks, will we see you there, at the wedding?" Jesse genuinely asked.

"Of course, I already have my invitation. Wouldn't miss this one for anything, one of my best friends getting married. This is a once in a lifetime event." Nicole labored her comments.

"Good to see you're doing so well, Nicole, we'll talk later." Catherine felt it was time to move on before something was said that shouldn't.

They found a table and ordered their drinks. As they were sipping their drinks, Catherine couldn't resist asking him something. "So, Jesse, why haven't you tried to get me into bed like all the other guys have?"

He coughed a little. "Because... they didn't...respect you or deeply care about you. I don't want you to feel used Catherine...and that's why I agreed to marry you." Jesse scarcely got the sentence out.

"Are you being straight with me? Because I heard that Christians aren't into sex."

"They most definitely are," Jesse said. "Only we wait until after marriage. Once marriage has taken place, God's for it and I'm for it."

She almost said, *we're never having sex,* but in a split second, she realized there was no need to be cruel. She knew that he wouldn't do anything to hurt her, and she didn't necessarily want to be malicious. Instead, she said. "I thought you were in a cult. But you're like the sweetest person I've ever met. You're so kindhearted, especially after what I did to you." Her voice broke as she tried to stop herself from crying. "But this love thing.... how can you be so sure?"

Jesse reached across the table, took Catherine's hand and looked straight into her eyes, "Catherine, I know this God thing is not *hip to you, but God gave me a love for you, like a parent gives their child security when they're frightened. That is why I'll be happy to be the father to your child. These are the things I'm sure of." Tears flowed down her cheeks. She was no longer in control of the relationship. This frightened her a little, and she tried to pull her hand away from his, but he squeezed tighter.

"I don't know if your feelings for me will ever change, or if our marriage will last more than a year," Jesse said," but I will give you all that I am for as long as we are together."

She wiped her nose. "I don't know how I feel. I do feel something for you, but I still hate the fact that I'm my dad's campaign pawn, and that my future has been taken away, and that I'm pregnant....... I was so in control, but now I'm a disaster." She lowered her head and started to cry.

Jesse took her hand again and said, "I'm sorry, Catherine. If I could undo your problem, I would. If I could take your grief, I would. But I know this, there is no future without forgiveness."

She sniffled. "I have made such a mess of my life."

"Oh, I can relate to that." Jesse said.

She giggled softly. "Why did you feel like you had to rescue me?"

He paused. ".....I know what it feels like to need rescuing. Not to sound all religious, but God rescued me, and He wanted me to help you."

She didn't say anything sarcastic. She only looked at him for a moment and then said, "Three months ago, I was sitting in the school café talking about.... manicures, spa days and guys on the football team. Now I'm sitting in Socrates talking about God, babies and forgiveness."

"That's because three months ago you didn't know God or forgiveness and now you do." Jesses continued.

"Somehow I feel like I should make amends, like in those movies when you see a priest flagellate themselves." Catherine lamented.

"All of us deserve to be punished, but God wants you to see his mercy and kindness. That's what he offers to all people, we're not special. To God, everybody is special and his gift of mercy is for all. We just have to accept it." Jesse answered animated.

"There was a time when the world was mine and I was queen of my realm, who would have thought my moral decisions would have crumbled my kingdom and be my undoing." This was new for Catherine, volunteering her weaknesses to be heard.

"Death to a world of our own making is actually a good thing. If we try to save our self-importance we will end up losing it, but if we lose our ego for a higher purpose we will find the real meaning of life." Jesse explained excitedly.

"But what higher purpose is there than my purpose?" Catherine confessed with a look of confusion on her face.

"God's purpose." Jesse ventured.

Catherine's world view was colliding with Jesse's love. Her liberal perspective had served her well, but what she was discovering was that Jesse's beliefs were all about others, not himself. His caring was a new kind of oxygen to her heart. She was finding these talks cathartic, helpful in a completely new way. Every conversation was used to promote her prospects, but these heart-to-hearts we're actually healing her soul. A part of her she was unfamiliar with.

Catherine looked down. "I need something from you," she said. "I need to know that you forgive me." She couldn't look at him because his answer could be too painful. She had never been so open with any other guy like this, and she had been trained by her dad to always keep the upper hand in every conversation.

Jesse reached over and cupped his hand over hers that was holding the drink, "Absolutely," he answered.

She looked up at him, her makeup a little smeared over her cheeks. "Thank you." she muttered.

There was a long pause until she began to laugh softly. "Can we go now? I can't be seen right now. I look terrible." Jesse nodded. They got up and walked out of the mall, towing about eight shopping bags. Once outside

Catherine changed the subject and asked, "So, what evil deeds have you done, Jesse? Or am I the only bad person here?"

"Ha. Uhhh... do you remember the huge food fight in the cafeteria last year?" Jesse asked.

"That was you?" Catherine said smiling.

"Yeah, Nick and I, we thought we'd leave our mark before we left high school."

"Oh, you definitely left a mark. You left a mark on my friend Ann's Yves Saint Laurent top. She had a meltdown!" Catherine explained.

Jesse laughed. "I'm not sorry."

"You better be glad it wasn't my top. I'd never forgive you." She hit him with several of her bags as she said it and then thought, *am I flirting with him?*

"Let's see, what else?...we also toilet papered Principal Adams' car in March of our final year. That was kinda cool." Jesse snickered.

Catherine giggled, "So, there is a dark side to you, Jesse Reynolds. She paused. "Hmmm... Catherine Reynolds. What do you think?"

Jesse grinned so wide he thought his face would crack. He had thought about that name non-stop since the day he had accepted his fate. He felt a rush through his body as he realized she was continuing to warm towards him. He abruptly realized he was hungry and asked Catherine, "Hey, I would kill for some pizza now, wanna join me?"

"Why not, I'm getting fat anyway." Catherine answered lightheartedly. "I might as well take advantage of it." The restaurant was on the other side of the shopping center.

* * * * *

Nicole had been observing Catherine and Jesse during their chat, and she was perplexed by the way Jesse was treating Catherine. Did she miss something, did Catherine accuse Jesse of getting her knocked up? Why was he being so understanding and affectionate? She was going to have to call

Hannah and find out what had happened while she was in the hospital and recovering. Jesse did not look like a victim to her.

Walking through the parking lot Jesse peered over at Catherine, "you have that serious face again." Catherine remarked.

"I have a serious face?" Jesse replied sheepishly.

"I saw it in my father's study that awful day." Catherine hazard a guess.

"Well, I do have something serious to say, when you named me as the partner in crime in your dad's office and he asked if I would marry you, I was well aware of the consequences to my reputation and future. As a matter of fact, God has actually warned me that I was going to suffer."

Catherine looked shocked, "you're saying that God is behind this?"

"No, he didn't cause this to happen, we humans are pro's at getting ourselves in trouble, we don't need God manipulating our misfortune. But he was simply preparing me for this day. What I'm saying is, I didn't know to what extent the fallout would be from the decisions that were made that day. I was fully expecting the worst to happen, to have my name smeared in the papers, loss of my reputation in church and being branded as a hypocrite." Jesse explained.

"And I was expecting my dad to shuttle me off to have an abortion, until his political imagination went wild." Catherine reasoned.

"But your dad has shielded both of us from what could have been ruin. Now I know he did it for selfish reasons but nonetheless, it has been a welcome relief. But there will come a time when we will be labeled, both among Christians and liberals. When we come back here a year from now, if we do return, or when our child is old enough to understand. But I wanted you to know, I made my decision in that study and I'm not going back, whatever the price." Jesse asserted.

"Yeah, and apart from my own personal torment it has been relatively painless. I only hope that I haven't put you through too much horror, it's something I'm regretting now that I know you. Looking back, my insensitivity was alarming." Catherine confessed with her head down. She glanced up contemplating his face in that moment, took hold of his arm with her two hands while leaning her head into his should whispering, "thank you." It was a nice moment until all the bags she was carrying interfered with their walking and they had to go back to using all four hands to carry everything.

"I hope this child is not a girl, we'll never have enough hands to carry all the clothes." Jesse laughed along with Catherine.

# CHAPTER 25

# THE WEDDING

*"Celebrate with me, friends! Raise your glasses—To life! To love!"*

*Solomon 5:1 MB*

Catherine's speech at the Leadership Institute symposium surprised everyone because she didn't sound self-absorbed or glitzy. She talked about sacrifice, overcoming broken dreams and the strength to change. She also never used the phrase, 'the future is pregnant with possibilities,' although her close friends were expecting it. Olivia, standing in the back was proud of Catherine, she had seen her girl grow up through all the trials of the summer. This was her final educational obligation at Danton University, and for Catherine, school was over, and so was her youth. The wedding day was fast approaching.

Relatives, out of state friends and guests were already beginning to arrive for the big event. It was pandemonium at the Stone's, entertaining guests, supervising wedding props, managing the extra hired staff at the house and calming Stan from the added stress of the wedding and media squall. His campaign however was soaring, the closer the wedding came the higher his polls rose. He was now 13 points in the lead, it was unprecedented. Catherine and Jesse's fairy tail romance had offered the people of the state a distraction from the recession, and Washington, they were impressed with the Governor's tactics.

Now it was here, the wedding day. It had only been a little over a month since Catherine had blamed Jesse in her father's study. And here she was, standing in front of the mirror looking at a woman she no longer knew. Her former life was like a phantom limb, severed off but still feeling lifelike. The endless arguments with her parents, the constant explaining to her close friends, all the silly advice from people on marriage - it all seemed so surreal to her. And now, here in her wedding dress... the most impromptu life event of all.

Her mom and her did have fun picking out the wedding dress, this gorgeous Japanese Mikado strapless gown. It had a natural waistline that was accentuated with exquisite crystal detailing with a flirty hip draping design. If she had to sacrifice her ambitions, she was at least going to do it with style.

But then there was Jesse, the solitary shinning figure of her life. He was the only one who was not a part of this whole sordid mess. And just when she thought he was making it harder by his decision to go along with it all, he turned out to be the one genial person. She could still hear him saying, "I'm sorry, Sir," to her father after being accused that day in the study. She remembered him commenting that her eyes were beautiful at the dance, and touching her chiffon dress at Sakes Fifth Avenue. Moments of kindness that seemed to affect her. She thought of other boys who had touched her, meaningless physical contact, and how she wished she could take some magical bath to wipe away all those memories. Jesse's small touches meant so much more. He was the quintessential of unselfishness, even altruistic in nature. *Am I falling in love with Jesse?* She thought.

"It's time, dear." Her mom said as she entered the room, followed by Jesse's mother. "Oh honey, you're beautiful. You'll be the bride of the year. I didn't realize how grown up you'd become."

Catherine laughed. "I just didn't think the transformation would happen this way." With that Jesse's mom leaned over toward Catherine and said into her ear, "You're a beautiful bride, and welcome to the family." Mrs. Reynolds then left the room to give the mother and daughter a few minutes alone. Catherine's eyes became moist with tears at the warmth of Mrs. Reynolds's words. She had never experienced such magnanimity from her family where everything was tainted by some angle or ulterior motive.

Catherine's mom broke into Catherine's thoughts, "We both know how daddy can be such a tyrant at times, especially when it comes to his political career. But you have handled everything so well, my darling girl."

"Thanks, mom," she said. "I know this has been torture on everybody." Catherine played with her bouquet.

"I'm sure that, in time, daddy and I will forgive Jesse for what he did. He has put all of us in a very compromising position and cost us a bundle of money too. But you know your father, he's a virtuoso at turning enemies into colleagues." Her mom paused and asked, "By the way, you have never told me how you feel about Jesse?"

"Feel?" asked Catherine.

"Yes, you know, love, hate, indifference or.......anything?" Her mom knew this was a difficult time, and was hoping that something positive was happening in her daughter. .

Catherine blushed. Her mouth went dry. "What a question to ask at this moment! I... I.... don't know," she stammered.

"Well, that's better than loathing him." her mother said. "Now. Let's put on our happy faces and brave the lions."

In the other part of the Stone's house were the bridesmaids, Beth and Ann, Hannah and Nicole squeezing into their Dessy gowns. The dress's had a delicate curved neckline framing a snug fitting bodice with animated fabric to create a flared mermaid skirt at the dropped waistline. It was a full-length gown revealing the arms and upper back. The girls were squealing and joking, pulling and tucking themselves into their dresses. When they finished Nicole asked, "I saw Jesse and Catherine at the Socrates coffee cafe and Jesse didn't look like an accused victim who's been unjustly condemned, did I miss something from our last talk at Catherine's house?"

"Yes," Hannah ventured, "fate tipped her hand in another direction. Believe it or not, Jesse accepted the blame for Catherine's scheme, then her dad came up with the ruse to have them marry because he thought it would win him the election."

"It looks like that part has worked." Beth jumped in.

"And to all of our surprise, it looks like Jesse's compassionate heart is changing our Catherine, it looks like she's falling in love with him, from what I can see." Hannah said.

"That's what I saw as well," Nicole repeated, "it was clear that Jesse was steering the relationship and not Catherine, and that's just not her style."

"You should have seen them at the dance, it was a sweep you off your feet kiss that we witnessed." Ann conveyed.

"Do you think Jesse really loves her?" Nicole asked.

"Catherine told us that Jesse said he loved her, only not romantic love but a religious love." Beth related.

"What does that mean?" Nicole questioned.

"I don't know, but if Christians call it religious love and we call it romance, I want some of it, because to me it looks like the real thing." Hannah chimed in, and the other two girls agreed.

As Catherine, her mom and the bridesmaids came walking out of the house to climb into the limousines, Ted's girlfriend who was waiting outside came running up to Catherine and asked if she could speak to her for just a moment. She was Ann's cousin and had just recently joined their inner circle. Catherine walked over to her while the rest of the wedding party scrambled into the cars.

"I know the truth Catherine, the whole truth about you and Ted, and why you're getting married so quickly," but before she could finish Catherine broke in saying, "what are you talking about and why are you confronting me with this now, of all days."

"Ted is having a nervous breakdown about him being the possible father of your baby and that this story will come out and ruin his family's reputation. Now I don't know what your father is up too, but some journalist tried to blackmail him into telling a story for the newspaper." Angie related franticly.

"This is the first I've heard of this and I'll talk to my dad about it and get back to you." Catherine said reassuringly.

"Tell me the truth Catherine, is Ted the father and are you pregnant?" Angie asked desperately.

Catherine lied, "No, now you, Ted and his family have nothing to worry about, I give you my word. I'm getting married because I'm... in.............love." Catherine's universe stood still as her words echoed in her heart slowly reregistering with her conscious thought, as though her soul spoke for her and not herself.

Angie gazed up into her face and said, "You maybe able to tell from my tone that I'm the jealous type, which is why I'm infuriated that you maybe carrying my boyfriends baby. And because of what I know of you, I don't believe you, I'm going to confront your father today at the reception and see what he has to say about all of this. I just wanted to hear you deny it, which is exactly what I expected. And I believe your father will pay me big money to keep this story out of the papers." Now it became clear what Angie was up to, blackmail, and why had she timed it just at this moment when she knew Catherine and her dad couldn't do anything about it.

"I'm sorry, but I must be going, I'll talk to you at the wedding." Catherine excused herself and bundled into the car.

The Governor had hired the City Lutheran Church that resembled a small cathedral, with spirals, stained glass windows, high pulpits and massive wooden doors. The church was made of double-height brick and stone. It had a pitched slate roof, and was famous for having a ceramic mosaic behind the altar, and painted decorative organ frontal pipes in the back of the sanctuary. The nave and clerestory windows, which feature St. Peter preaching at Jerusalem and Christ returning in glory with angels, ushering in a reign of peace was the real show piece of the church.

As Catherine, her mom and the wedding party walked into the church, it was full to overflowing. Anyone who was someone was there, it was the who's who of the region. Jim and Andy were on the two sides of the entrance,

Olivia was standing to the right of the sanctuary on the left hand side because it gave the best view of the alter area. Senator Colin, Senator Edward, James, Joshua, Steven Forger the campaign manager and Monet were all seated together to witness the finality of their machinations. Coco was sitting on her own, since Nicole was in the wedding party, looking abandoned and heartbroken. Philip the detective was also there because of how he handled Nicole's case, but since then he had been recruited by the FBI for the work he did in cracking the international smuggling ring. Catherine had invited him as a kindness to Nicole. Ted and his girlfriend, along with his parents were sitting toward the front because his parents were large contributors to the Governor's campaign. But Ted was clearly suffering from hypertension over his blackmail ordeal. On Jesse's side there was Pastor Greg and Mary Sutton, the evangelist. She came to witness the suffering beauty, Catherine. The worship team and many of his church friends were there as well as his grandmother, who he adored.

Jesse was standing up front at the alter with his best man Nick, looking back for the moment when the bridesmaids and groomsmen entered the sanctuary with Catherine following with her dad. The music started by a string quartet dressed in tuxedos'. The music filled the high ceiling chamber producing perfect acoustics, it sounded angelic as the wedding party started walking down the aisle.

As the bridesmaids and groomsmen were walking down the isle, Catherine had to warn her dad about Angie. This was her moment of truth because she felt the truth could come out and she would rather it came from her than someone else. "Dad, I know this is not the right time but I have something shocking to tell you, Catherine whispered, "this baby I'm having, it's not Jesse's. He's not the father, he never took advantage of me or even touched me."

Stan glared at Catherine as they both began walking down the aisle with his arm interlocking with her arm. "Then why did you accuse Jesse of being the culprit?" And why did he agree to marry you?" Her father asked incensed.

"I wanted to get an abortion, and I thought that if I accused a Christian, which you hate, that you would have sent me away and arranged for a secret abortion. I was afraid to go myself thinking that if the papers found out it would have ruined your election chances. But I was as surprised as you are now that Jesse agreed to marry me, that was never my idea nor desire." Catherine explained.

"Are you destined to destroy my career, your taking me from one frying pan to another." Her dad murmured.

People could hear them talking in hushed tones with animated intensity wondering if something was wrong, even though Catherine and her dad were smiling behind their gritted teeth.

"I just wanted to warn you because Ted's girlfriend, the guy whose baby I am having is going to confront you at the reception and you need to act surprised and deny her allegations. She's trying to blackmail you into paying for her silence." Catherine asked

"At least I can see you're still my daughter, scheming and plotting things to work to your advantage. I am proud of that." And with that her dad had brought her up to the alter.

The aisle they had just walked down was laid with a white carpet having small classic birdcage lantern's with live candles and elegant white blooming flowers on each pew that led to the altar. The flower girl, Jesse's sister, sprinkled rose petals before them and could hear Catherine and her dad speaking in hushed tones.

When they arrived at the altar, the Minister said, "Who gives this woman to be married?"

In his garish way, the Governor answered, "I'm paying for this wedding, so I do." The people laughed nervously.

Jesse took Catherine's hand and helped her up to the next step, where they stood facing each other. Her emerald eyes were jewel-like, exquisite. *She just gets more and more beautiful,* Jesse thought. She was his diva queen, and so much more. She wore her hair up with french curls, showing off her graceful, swanlike neck. She was chic and elegant in every way. Jesse's eyes were a warm blue – inviting, understanding and strong. And in his black tuxedo, he looked *boss to her.

They exchanged their vows and their wedding rings. As they said, "I do," they each felt a small shiver go through their bodies. The minister then said, "You may now kiss the bride."

As their lips pressed against each others, Catherine's heart began to pound. Her cheeks became flushed, her eyes flew open wide and she pushed herself back from Jesse. Her mom gasped aloud, while Jesse and the whole congregation hung in suspense.

"Jesse," Catherine whispered, so only he could hear, "I know how I feel! I love you." Than she backed up and yelled it: "I LOOOVE YOU!!" She threw her arms around his neck and kissed him again. The audience cheered and clapped. Jesse wrapped his arms around her, picked her up off her feet and said, "I love you, Catherine, and I always will."

When everything settled down, the Minister asked politely if he could continue with the ceremony. Everybody laughed, especially Jesse's parents. The minister said his final remarks. " As you leave here today, there is one thing that will ensure a successful marriage. John 15:13 in the Bible says, 'Greater love has no one than this, that he lay down his life for his friends.' If the two of you will live by this rule, putting the other person first, you'll be blessed. There are different kinds of love, romantic love is what most people enjoy, and it certainly warms the heart with passion. But there is a greater kind of love called agape, this is unconditional love. This is what God showed us while his Son Jesus was being crucified, in his suffering and injustice he prayed for the very ones who were killing him, 'Father, forgive them, for they know not what they do.' This is the kind of love that continues to love even when the other person does not deserve it. And this is the kind of love that will create a bond in marriage that cannot be broken."

As Catherine heard those words while looking into Jesse's eyes, she had her own *eureka moment that, that was how Jesse loved her: he was laying down his life, his plans, his future, his reputation – everything she had been so unwilling to give up - all for her. And now, Jesse's love had led her to real love. She threw her arms around Jesse and kissed him again speaking in-between the kisses, "I believe Jesse, I believe." Jesse's parents were crying, the Minister was smiling, the crowd was going wild because of all the skepticism and rumors that surrounded this couple they were now being dispelled as they saw Catharine kissing Jesse with abandonment. The photographers and journalists were loving this. And Hannah was saying, "he is a dreamboat," to the other bridesmaids around her. Spontaneously, Nick started singing, 'My true love.....', then the other groomsmen joined in, then the bridesmaids, the string quartet picked it up and soon the whole crowd was singing.

Nicole was realizing simultaneously with Catherine the difference between religious love and romantic love. What she and her friends were talking about in the bridesmaids room. She bowed her head and said, "God, I don't know you, I was even angry at you for my cursed life. But if you can give me this kind of love, I'll believe in you too, and I'll forgive my dad and mom for the things they have done to me and to each other."

The Governor was standing there with everybody else as they all sang, but he wasn't singing, he wasn't celebrating, he was seething. Jesse had won his daughter over while he was conspiring to marginalize Jesse's faith. Now Jesse had taken his daughter away from him, which meant Jesse just became a liability to his progress for the White House. Something was going to have to be done. The Governor should have known, if it looks like peace, then it means someone is planning war. Jesse may not have known it, but he just declared war with his father-in-law.

At the reception, it was Nick's turn to give a speech. He stood up and raised his glass of Ariel Blanc, a fine non alcoholic wine because so many of the wedding party and guess were under 21, while the over 21's raised their glasses of champaign for the toast. Nick shared several stories of Jesse's life with a few cliffhangers that bordered on embarrassment but keep it safe because of all the press. Then he ended it with, "I've known Jesse a long time, and I've known Catherine from a far for a long time, and I must say, over these past few months I have seen Jesse, a student of no consequence, become a knight, and Catherine, our resident drama queen, become a woman of substance." The place erupted with cheers and smiles. Nick had tears in his eyes and Hannah, Beth, Ann and Nicole were also misting up. Amy, Jesse's sister ran over to him and gave him a big hug that went over well with the audience.

After the speeches were over and everybody was eating, Angie tried to talk to the Governor but he kept himself protected from her. He would deal with her later.

Marry Sutton, the evangelist, felt impressed of the Lord to talk to Nicole. She went over to her and asked if she could pray for her. As they prayed Nicole gave her heart to the Lord with many tears. For the first time in her life she felt an indescribable peace, as if all of her anger, bitterness and fears fell off of her heart like a backpack. Was she actually experiencing God? She saw the effect God had on Catherine's life, everybody at the wedding could see it also, now it was her turned. It was true what Mary was telling her, God did love her. Is this what love feels like? After so many years of longing for love it came not from her parents but from an unseen God. How could she not forgive her parents, this kind of love could change them as well. And with Mary still next to her, she forgive her father and mother.

The photographs had been taken, the reception was winding down and it was time for Jesse and Catherine to leave for their honeymoon. Everybody gathered outside on the path that lead to their getaway car, Catherine's Thunderbird. They came out of their changing rooms and made their way to the doors holding hands like two little kids going off to Disneyland. Everybody was ready with handfuls of rice, but when they reached the doors, Jesse pulled Catherine close to him and kissed her with a strong embrace. Cheers erupted, Hanna swooned and Nick was looking up at God saying, "could you give me a girl like Catherine without the white knuckle ride."

In the small idyllic village of Gerberoy, Jonathan was listening to the live radio broadcast and missing Nicole and his wife Coco as he sat at his local French cafe sipping coffee. Even though he was surrounded by half timber houses, French style gardens and charming cobble stone streets that once attracted post- impressionist artist, he was feeling some regret. The scars on his face would forever be a reminder of his abuse to his daughter. Having time on his hands was putting him in touch with some feelings he was uncomfortable with.

* * * * *

Jesse and Catherine were now in England, and after orientation and meeting with their professors at Oxford they registered with the National Health Service for Catherine to have here first baby examine. Hannah started attending Jesse's church manhunting for her dreamboat, believing that if Catherine could get one so could she. Nicole was also going with her now that she felt like a reborn person. Nick, who met them at the wedding would sit with them and thought maybe God was answering his prayer for a babe. To everyone in church the two girls looked like babes and all the other guys were envious. Beth and Ann had their short movie accepted into the New York film festival and were setting their sights on Hollywood. And Olivia, she developed a phobia of duct tape and decided to switch to an Ford. And the Governor, he was turning more and more to the dark side now that it was certain he would win the election and Jesse had taken his daughter away. Glenn was getting lost in the latest version of video games in Florida and quickly developing a good case of paranoia. Ted's airhead girlfriend was still thinking she could blackmail the Governor with the possible rumor of Catherine's pregnancy. She spent her time drawing stick figures to illustrate her blackmail notes.

But the real story was of Jesse and Catherine and how love won the day.

# THE END

Printed in Great Britain
by Amazon

24963021R00116